TU-KIN

TU-KIN

ERGENE-KON

SEYFI CINAR

Cover design by: Zen Toronto
Printed in the United Kingdom

The author dedicates this book to all Turkic people from around the world.

CONTENTS

THE EMPIRE

This story begins with the reign of İl-Han, descendant of the great Oguz-Khan, who ruled the Great Hunnic Empire and saw no parallel amongst his contemporaries. İl-Han held the same power and might as his ancestors, and so continued to overpower his enemies and expand the empire even further than his forefathers. He was also able to eliminate the rebellion of many bordering enemies and secure their trust, leaving few able to stop him. With all of his successes, İl-Han's lust for power began to multiply. As he continued to defeat his rivals and add to his dominion, evils began to emerge within him, hell-bent on corrupting his heart.

İl-Han was soon intoxicated by his victories. The evil spirits within had succeeded in gaining control over his conscience and led him down a dark path. Those who were defeated were now given an ultimatum, join İl-Han's empire or face humiliation and execution in front of thousands of onlookers.

During his reign of terror, İl-Han's army defeated that of one of his sworn enemies, the Tatars. In his arrogance, he believed that the fallen clan of warriors would easily surrender to his might, after he had once again become victorious. Reality, however, was entirely different from what he thought. There was much more to the Tatars than what met the eyes. After their defeat, they forcefully bowed to the king and yielded by swearing their allegiance to him, but, deep down, their hearts burned with the want for revenge. The Tatars were known far and wide for their barbarism, viciousness, and ferocity. Failure was never an option in their way of life. The defeat drove them crazy as they eagerly looked for a chance to seize the throne and mercilessly defeat and destroy İl-Han's empire.

As time passed, the hatred the Tatars felt for İl-Han grew deeper and İl-Han himself added fuel to the fire as he beheaded one of their chiefs and tied the second in command to one of his chariots, who eventually died of the torment. This mockery was hard to accept for the proud barbarians, and so the Tatars swore to avenge their chiefs. They began to secretly extend their connections to the Kyrgyz tribe, as well as other enemies of İl-Han, all of whom had been brought to their knees by his ever expanding empire. They were initially hesitant to give their support to Sevinc-Han, the only remaining chief of the Tatars, as they had sworn allegiance to İl-Han. They were all well aware of the might of İl-Han and did not have enough courage to revolt.

Nonetheless, Sevinc-Han eventually succeeded in convincing them and promised them high ranks within the soon-to-be conquered empire. The rebellion would soon begin. The Tatars understood the fact that İl-Han could not be overthrown in battle, but instead by deception. Hence, they decided to commence the rebellion by corrupting those close to him.

İl-Han, oblivious of what lay ahead of him, held a large feast in celebration of his latest victory. He had three sons, all of whom had inherited his vigour. They were named KorHan, KulHan, and KayHan. Out of the three, the youngest son, KayHan, surpassed the other two in courage and fearlessness. İl-Han loved his son for his traits, and labelled him the Lion of the Turks.

Little did İl-Han know, however, that many of his most trusted allies present at the feast had already decided to betray him and side with the Tatars in the rebellion. Taking full advantage of the change in allegiances, the Tatars advanced in implementing their evil strategies.

Through any means necessary, the Tatars managed to turn different Turkic groups against each other. They left no stone unturned in bringing about chaos throughout the land, continuing to damage the roots of İl-Han's empire. Sevinc-Han, along with his allies, invaded and put an end to İl-Han's already declining rule. He had been seemingly invincible, yet he lost his life during the war, and his once magnificent reign came to an end. Though the Tatars had succeeded in overthrowing İl-Han, their anger kept burning. Their rage led to them brutally killing every man, woman and child in the empire, setting their homes on fire and aiming to wipe out the entire population that had lived under İl-Han's rule.

Their mission had been fulfilled. İl-Han and his tribe had been demolished, and those who had managed to escape hid in places that were distant from the rising sun. The Tatars believed that the lineage of İl-Han had been eradicated, and that there would not be any threat from their side in the future. History, however, would not see it that way. It would soon give rise to a legend. A legend that would restore the might and honour of the lost Turkic empire.

THE ESCAPE

"**H**urry up, Tilbe! We must get out of here now!" KayHan said to his wife, as the fire raged outside of their tent, "They have sieged the entire encampment, we will die if we do not leave right now!"

His tone was filled with terror despite his best attempts to remain calm. Though he was a man of courage, the danger approaching him and his remaining family had caused him to panic. He had already lost both of his dear brothers as well as his beloved father. He had been devastated by the losses. A storm of emotions surged inside of him, but there was nothing he could do to undo the destruction. His left arm was bleeding profusely, and his body was covered in multiple scars from the invaders' attack, but he had no time to think about the pain in his arm, nor the pain in his heart.

The entrance to his home opened and in stepped Berkan, one of his loyal servants and childhood friends.

"The horses are ready my prince!" He announced, "We must leave immediately, before the invaders get closer. I have already spoken to Nukuz. He has done all of the necessary preparations. Your children will be safe with him."

The two had watched each other's backs since they were young boys, and their friendship remained firm in this time of peril. Berkan had been ordered to arrange the horses for the prince, his cousin Nukuz, and their families. KayHan listened to him and silently decided on what he must do. He beckoned at Tilbe to take hold of their children and leave immediately with Berkan. Perplexed, Tilbe rushed towards him and held his hands gently in her own.

"What do you mean by that? Surely you are not serious? I refuse to leave without you. There is no life for us without you. Do you hear me? We will not leave, and that is final."

KayHan looked at her in a mix of concern and care. Her loving but confused eyes looked back. He cupped her face in his hands in order to try and assure her that everything would be okay. He wanted to tell her a lot of things. How he had felt when he first laid eyes on her, how he had spent the best days of his life with her, how the birth of his children had made him the happiest man on earth. And yet, his worry prevented him from expressing himself. He continued to stare at her face for a few moments before wiping her tears with his hands.

"You are the best thing that ever happened to me and I will make sure I come back to see you again."

Saying this, he turned to his children, kissed them both on their cheeks, and rushed out of the tent, paying no heed to Tilbe's objections. Tilbe ran towards him and attempted to call him back, but KayHan continued on. He had no choice but to leave. There was something he had to do. Berkan tried his best to comfort Tilbe but tears continued to pour down her face.

Once her tears had finally subsided, Tilbe came to her senses. She wrapped her arms around her children, holding them tight to her chest, and followed Berkan out of the tent toward the secret pathway that had been specifically made beforehand for situations such as the one they were currently in.

As they reached the secret passage, they found Nukuz and his wife already waiting there for them. Nukuz was KayHan's cousin, and, despite being as headstrong and determined as his brethren, he too was worried about the danger his family were in. Both he and his wife, Abay, were close to KayHan's own family, and so they were relieved to see Tilbe emerge in front of them with her children. As Tilbe arrived, Abay rushed over to hug her, the two of them crying profusely. They both understood the pain they were in, being subject to the destruction of both their village, and those who lived alongside them.

"Where is KayHan?" Abay asked in concern.

"I... I do not know," Tilbe responded, "He told me that he had to go somewhere, but he did not tell me what exactly he had to do."

"I am sure KayHan will come back to us safe," Nukuz affirmed, "For now we must follow Berkan and make sure we get to safety ourselves."

With Nukuz's word, Berkan proceeded to show them the pathway. As they traversed the passageway, each of them remembered the time they had spent with their murdered friends and family. Tilbe failed to stop thinking about KayHan. She was unable to think of how she could live her life without him.

She eventually refused to imagine a future without KayHan at her side. She continued holding her children tightly, kissing them at regular intervals along the way. Though she tried her hardest to refrain from crying even more, she was unable to stop more tears from dripping down her cheeks.

Reaching the end of the secret path, they could see a group of horses situated ahead of them, each one very visibly prepared for them to escape on. Nukuz ordered everyone to mount the horses immediately, but Tilbe's eyes constantly looked back at the path they had come from, wishing with all her might for KayHan to appear. Nukuz understood the trauma she must have been experiencing and walked over to her. She looked at him, the worry etched over her face.

"When will KayHan join us?" She asked in fear.

Nukuz did not have a solid answer for her, but he knew he had to comfort her in order for Tilbe to be able to continue.

"He will be behind us before you know it. But we must not wait here anymore, it is not safe here. He will catch up to us in the mountains."

Hearing this, Tilbe felt a wave of hope flow through her. Without wasting any more time, Tilbe handed one of her children over to Berkan, who placed her child in front of him on his horse. She then climbed her own horse, making sure her other child was securely sat on the steed's back, and instructed it to run. The small group slowly but surely made its way towards the giant, snowy mountains. Throughout the journey, they were constantly filled with the terror of being caught and brutally slaughtered. The sight of their clan's homes burning to ashes from a distance, as well as the very audible screams of those failing to escape, did nothing to lighten the mood.

Fate was not as kind to KayHan compared to his wife and children. It had decided to test him even more. As soon as KayHan had left, he had headed towards his father's tent. He had loved his father just as much as Tilbe and his children, and so he refused to leave without bidding him a final farewell.

He entered İl-Han's tent with his heart aching. The grief of losing almost his entire family caused him to cover his face with his hands and cry for a few moments. He wanted to cry more, but he knew it was unwise to linger over past memories when danger was still at large. He soon heard a few footsteps from outside the tent, their sound increasing in volume with each passing second. He quickly hid behind a large curtain, hoping those nearing were allies and not enemies. The footsteps soon stopped as KayHan heard the tent entrance open. Voices then proceeded to fill the tent, KayHan recognizing them as belonging to two of his father's courtiers. Relieved that he was no longer in immediate danger, KayHan revealed himself. The two figures in front of him were shocked to see him. The prince, however, paid no attention to their surprise and started speaking to them.

"Ayi and Mir. I am glad to see the two of you. I was almost scared to death. I came here to retrieve my family's heirloom, it must not be held by anyone other than a member of my family. It is my right to keep it, as I am the true heir to this throne. I know that we have been defeated today, but I am sure that tomorrow we can reclaim this land. I will return to this throne soon enough. Now help me in finding it."

KayHan knew the two as loyal and obedient servants that would obey his orders without hesitation, but the two did not act upon his instruction.

"Did you not hear your prince?" KayHan questioned in confusion, "Help me find my family's heirloom."

"We are sorry, KayHan," Ayi responded, "We will get to it now."

"Of course," Mir added, "We will do everything in our power to make sure our leader claims what is his."

Though the words were friendly, KayHan could tell something was wrong. He could sense defiance within the courtiers' voices, and a sneering look had plastered itself over their faces. Almost certain that he was now in the immediate danger he had previously thought was dispelled, KayHan quietly placed his hand around the hilt of his blade. In a flash, KayHan dodged to his side, managing to avoid a swing of Mir's sword by the skin of his teeth. That was when he understood. They were indeed making sure their leader claimed what was theirs. He now knew, however, that he was no longer their leader. KayHan had hardly brought himself out of the grief of losing his family, and yet he was now in a fight against the two traitors.

The two had caught KayHan off-guard, and they initially gained the upper hand on the prince, Ayi succeeding in wounding his shoulder. Though they outnumbered him, there was a reason Ayi and Mir had been nothing but courtiers beforehand, and KayHan soon fought back. Managing to evade and parry the rest of the traitors' attacks, KayHan easily defeated the two former courtiers, who were now both dead on the floor in front of him. Now that the perpetrators had been dealt with, KayHan recommended his search of the tent. Fortunately for the prince, the search was a short one and he eventually found his family's heirloom. It was an opal pendant, composed of several rare blue stones, each one baring ancient Turkic inscriptions.

Leaving his father's tent, KayHan wanted to fulfil one more wish before he could return to his awaiting family, no matter how careless it seemed. He desperately wanted to see his father and his brothers once more before he left them forever. He knew retrieving a horse at this time was impossible unless he wished to die trying. He was already severely wounded, and he knew one more ambush would finish him off. Despite this, his will never wavered. Nothing could stop the determination of a man fighting for his family, and though KayHan had lost his brothers and father, his wife and children were still eagerly awaiting his return. He had to succeed for their sake.

Passing over the many dead bodies of those slaughtered by the Tatars, he tried his best to remain out of their sight. Scanning the area for the corpses of his father and brothers, he could feel his heart pounding against the inside of his chest. Suddenly, he became paralyzed, his eyes were filled with horror and dismay, the sight he looked upon sending a shudder down his spine. It was his father's corpse. It felt as if his soul had deserted his body. The power from his legs faded entirely as he dropped to his knees in despair.

The sweet memories of his family started flowing through his brain once again. All the stories he had been told, all the meals he had eaten alongside him and all the love he had felt. He knew all of these were now gone. His hands began trembling as he held his father's head and rested it on his lap, the blood from his father's wounds soaking his clothes as he did so. The thought of a day like this had never crossed KayHan's mind before, but it had come to be in tragic fashion. He gazed upon his father's face for a while longer before he kissed his forehead.

As he turned his father's dead body to its side, he was horrified to see that his corpse had been mutilated, his hands had been cut off and his body scarred all over. The Tatars had avenged their chiefs well. They failed to leave a single jewel on the body of the murdered king. Though KayHan could feel his grief and anger clashing within him, he had no time to cry beside the dead body nor was he able to bury it. He gently placed the body back in its former position and left for the mountains. He remembered his remaining family and how they were still waiting for his return. He could do nothing to stop the massacre of that day, but KayHan made a promise to himself that he would survive and see his wife and children once again.

He soon arrived at the secret pathway and ventured through it. Emerging from the other side, he retrieved the horse that Nukuz had left for him. His heart remained heavy with the ruin that the empire now resembled, and his soul was hurt by the loss of his brothers and father. His body was lined with several deep wounds, severely hindering his mobility. Ordering his horse to set off, he headed towards the mountains. The air-piercing screams of his people echoed around him as his horse galloped on.

The future looked hopeless, but KayHan reassured himself. Though the empire no longer existed, he knew that he was still its rightful king. Most of his family had been brutalized, but yet he remained alive, determined to restore the rule of his lineage. The journey back to reclaiming the empire would be the hardest thing he or his people could achieve, but he was certain, whether it be him or one of his descendants, that his clan would return to their lost empire and rule over it once again.

There was no certainty that KayHan would reach his remaining family, and so he had to be careful throughout the rest of his venture up the mountain. The howling winds and dark skies promised a difficult time for him in his venture, but the thought of his wife and children allowed him to power on.

ERGENE-KON

A top one of the mountains, Tilbe eagerly awaited her husband's presence, for which the hope among the group remained high. Nukuz and Abay had remained with her and her children, wanting to ensure their safety. They had made a fire in order to keep the group warm in the snowy conditions, yet Tilbe continued to wait away from it. She knew of KayHan's fighting ability, but she was also well aware of the danger that he could have encountered. His safety was not a guarantee, and that was what scared her.

"Tilbe! Come and join us!" Abay called over from the fire, "You should have some food. You have not eaten anything since yesterday."

Tilbe's gaze did not move from the path down the mountain, but she responded.

"I will eat in a little while, please continue without me."

It was evident that she had lost her appetite out of worry, but Abay knew something to eat or drink would help in calming down her friend.

She neared Tilbe and stood beside her with a cup of hot tea.

"Here, have some."

Tilbe reluctantly received the cup and took a sip from it, her eyes fixated on the path. Abay stared at her for a moment before gazing at the sky and breaking the silence.

"Tilbe, I know this has been hard on you, and I do not want you to give up hope, but we do not know if KayHan will ever return."

The words frightened Tilbe, causing her to stop drinking her tea.

"I cannot think that way. I... I..."

She wanted to continue, but the words were caught up in her throat. Abay placed a comforting arm around her shoulders.

"Tilbe, my dear, think about your children. They still have their entire lives ahead of them and you need to play a big part in those lives. They need you to pull yourself together and move on alongside them. I know KayHan would not be happy to see his children suffering, especially after all he did to save them. He wanted them to have a better future and did all he could to make sure they have the opportunity to have that future. You must not let his efforts be in vain like this. I know that it will be hard on them to continue after losing one of their parents to war, but please make sure they do not lose another one to grief. You should take some time to think about it, but we must leave now. By the time the sun shines on us once again, we may be vulnerable to the Tatars. I know that you will make the right decision. You know very well that it is unwise to linger over the past at this time."

Her words were sharp but Tilbe knew she was telling the truth. Her eyes finally left the path and set themselves upon her two children, who were both eating at the fire. They were oblivious to the circumstances of their surroundings, but the sight of them caused Tilbe to calm down. She had to make sure they survived the ordeal they had no right to be a part of.

"I understand. Let us leave immediately. We should hurry before the Tatars find us."

A seemingly unending chaos had been deep inside of her ever since she had been separated from her husband, but Tilbe had to ignore it if she were to bring herself and her children to safety. Abay's words, though frosty, had shown her the gravity of the situation. Nukuz beckoned at Berkan, who instantly got to his feet and hastened the saddles to the horses.

Tilbe helped Abay in collecting the luggage, proceeding with the task as quick as she could in case of any unwanted attention from the Tatars was nearby. Nukuz and his wife climbed quickly onto their horses and waited for Tilbe to do the same. As she got on the horse, she turned back in the saddle, casting one final glance to the path behind them. Knowing that she had to leave KayHan behind, she finally decided to leave. No sooner had she returned her focus to the journey ahead when the group noticed a cloud of dust rising from behind them. Berkan and Nukuz quickly drew their swords out of their sheaths in preparation for an attack. The sound of gallops continued to increase in volume as the seconds went by, possibly the final seconds that the group would experience in their lives.

Soon enough a figure came into view from behind the cloud of dust. Berkan raised his sword at the sight.

"Do not come near us, or I will tear you limb from limb."

Berkan's voice contained a mix of ferocity and fear, but as the silhouette's true self came to light, the entire group exploded into happiness.

"You could never raise your sword against me, Berkan, you swore! Did you not?"

It was KayHan himself, sat atop his horse in front of them, bearing multiple wounds but, crucially, alive. Acknowledging the prince, the group's faces were filled with joy. Tilbe quickly returned to her feet and rushed over to her husband. The two embraced one another, their hug lasting a short while as the rest of the group climbed off their horses to greet KayHan. The returning prince was overjoyed to see his family and friends, who had been subject to so much death beforehand, alive and well. KayHan hugged his children as Nukuz treated his wounded shoulder, wrapping it in cloth in order to stop its bleeding. Once he had been tended to, the group began to plan for the next task. They had to find a place to reside where they could be safe, an area hidden from the Tatars.

"KayHan, we do not have anywhere to go apart from back to the empire, but we will die if we step foot there." Nukuz explained in dismay.

KayHan understood Nukuz's worry, but he still had hope.

"Nukuz, we have been through so much in this life, and yet, we are still here together. I am hopeful that we will find a safe home soon. All we need to do is to maintain our spirits."

The group nodded in agreement before beginning to move forward in the search that seemed never-ending, due to there being no visible passages amidst the snowy mountains. As they ventured around the many mountaintops, the feeling that their journey would not have a happy end started to creep into their minds. Dark storm clouds began forming in the sky as the wind became stronger, increasing their worry. Despite this, none of them wanted to give up on the search. Though it was not clear at first, fate had a special surprise waiting for them, and their will to continue on their search allowed them to encounter the gift they had been given. A herd of goats were soon visible in the near distance, an odd sight at such a high altitude and in such cold conditions.

Nukuz quickly pointed towards the herd.

"Look over there. A herd of goats! They must have a place to graze. We should follow them, they might lead us somewhere. It is a lot better than going around in circles."

There were some concerns in the minds of the group over following the herd, but the ever increasing number of dark clouds plaguing the sky made them agree with the plan. After following the goats for a while, they were led into a long and narrow path, almost invisible because of the snow. Then, to their utmost surprise, the goats disappeared mysteriously into the side of the mountain one after another. It was hard to make out from a distance, and of course, hard to believe, since there was no visible passage for a goat to pass through. They were unable to understand what had happened, and so they went closer in an attempt to see it.

As they all did so, a deafening thunder was heard. The immense sound from it was enough to cause a small portion of the snow from atop the mountain to collapse. The small avalanche came rushing down past them at an extraordinary speed, nearly crushing them with its monstrous force. KayHan covered the children with himself to shield them from the icy shower. The snow went crashing down the entire mountain, causing an ear-piercing sound amidst the dark and silent night.

The avalanche had stripped away many layers of snow, revealing a large opening to the passageway. This was no less than a miracle to the group. After all had finally settled down, they recollected their thoughts and brushed the snow from their clothes. Once they made sure that they were all safe and unharmed, they approached the opening and were grateful to see it lead into a pathway heading into what seemed to be the centre of the mountaintop.

Despite their happiness to see the newly opened passage, they could not help but have a sense of worry creep into their minds. The passage was quite a distance and it was still too dark for them to see its end. Nothing was said for a short period before KayHan finally took a step forward.

"This passage is what the herd of goats must have used to enter the mountain so it should be safe. It is dark, however, so we cannot see all the way to the other side, and your safety is my main priority. I will go in alone to ensure it is clear to trek. You should all wait for me until I return."

The group reluctantly agreed as they watched the prince advance through the opening. He slowly faded into the dark passageway. They anxiously awaited his return for what felt like ages, the first signs of sunlight had even emerged from behind the mountains.

"We cannot wait any longer, it has been far too long," said Tilbe frantically, "Something must have happened to him, we have to go after him now."

Without waiting for a response, Tilbe grabbed her horse's leash and entered the passageway. In fear of losing Tilbe as well, the others had no choice but to quickly follow. The passage was wide enough for their horses to fit but it was extremely sinuous and had jagged rocks protruding from the ground. They steadily advanced through the passage, slowed by their fear and uncertainty.

At long last they reached the end of the path, where they saw KayHan peering out into the open. Relieved to see him, Tilbe rushed over to embrace her husband. However as she neared him she saw the same sight that KayHan was looking at, and stopped where she stood.

"Look Tilbe," KayHan said softly, "Is it not beautiful?"

Tilbe was speechless as she gazed upon the awe-inspiring view. The rest of the group soon arrived at the scene before they too were taken aback by the sight. The passage had led them to the other side of the mountain, and they stared from atop the ledge.

There below them, was a valley that stretched to the edge of the horizon. Uneven hills that held up a mass number of bushes lined one side, while a wide forest, filled with thick vegetation, engulfed the other. The two were separated by a large lake that flowed over the middle of the valley. These were all surrounded by a range of steep, enormous mountains, each hosting a hair of snow on top.

After all of their misfortunes, they had finally been given a stroke of luck. The storm soon subsided and the morning sun emerged in all of its glory, lighting up the enchanted land that the passage led to. As they continued on to the captivating valley, what they encountered was even more rewarding. The land was filled with fruit trees and lush green plants alongside springs of fresh water and animals. They were star struck.

"Wow!" Tilbe exclaimed, beholding the beauty of the valley, "I cannot believe my eyes."

After a few more moments of admiration, KayHan turned to his companions.

"Listen, everyone." He explained, "This land looks to be safe. Come and behold how fate is kind on you today."

The fresh morning breeze stirred and the birds began chirping. Butterflies fluttered towards the newly blossomed buds while the bees buzzed away from their hives in search of nectar and pollen.

Taking in the ensnaring beauty of the valley, the onlookers remembered their ancestors as well as their lost loved ones while they were overcome with emotion. From the valley, the distant paramount snowy mountains could be seen clearly, covered with snow like velvet, standing with all their grandeur and making the enchanted valley all the more beautiful. KayHan's children started running around while the sounds of laughter echoed through the valley. They had started their journey escaping a war-torn empire that had been littered with corpses and flooded with blood, and now they were here, in an oasis that held nothing but beauty.

Nukuz and Abay walked over to the place where Tilbe and her husband were standing, watching their children playing happily in the lush fields.

"So is this where we shall stay from now on, for the rest of our lives? This place is wonderful. One can spend his entire life happily here," said Nukuz, "I fear the Tatars will never welcome us again in the empire. It would be best if we do not return to that land."

Abay nodded in agreement, but KayHan had other plans in his mind. He turned towards Nukuz, held him by the shoulders and looked straight into his eyes, wanting him to listen attentively.

"Nukuz, İl-Han was my father. He spent his entire life building that glorious empire, and there was no parallel to it. Nobody had the courage to confront us, and if it were not for those traitors, it would still be standing right now. I know it has fallen, but I have resolved to return and conquer it again to restore my ancestors' honour. I am the true heir to the throne."

Saying this, KayHan showed him the heirloom he had taken from İl-Han's tent before the Tatars could steal it.

"The separation from our homeland has been hard. I will never forget this cruelty, all that destruction at the hands of the Tatars. The cries and screams of those innocent people are still ringing in my head. I will return to my rightful land, Nukuz. I will return. I must return with glory, and regain the power and dignity that we once possessed. I will conquer the throne of my father again. Better days are waiting for us. The days when the sun will shine brighter than ever before, and that day will be the start of our new rule, our new reign."

Tilbe turned towards KayHan as he finished his speech with a broad smile on her face.

"Now that this is our home, I think we should name this valley," She stated, "So what do you think about it? What should we call it?"

KayHan smiled back at her.

"Why not decide the name yourself. We will all accept it willingly."

Tilbe was glad to have been given the honour of naming their new home.

"I think it should be named after these beautiful hills and tall mountains because they are essential to its beauty. It might sound a little odd, but I would like to make it a blend of two words, 'Ergene' and 'Kon'. That way it describes its arc shape as well as its high-rising mountains."

KayHan was surprised to see his wife so excited to name their new home, but he liked the sound of what she had come up with.

"Ergene-Kon," He said aloud, "I think it is perfect, how about you three?"

"It is perfect!" Abay responded, with Berkan and her husband nodding in agreement.

They all looked at the sky in gratitude. The calamity was over and they had been led to heaven. There was nothing more they could have asked for.

After KayHan and Nukuz, along with their families, settled in Ergene-Kon, they were exalted to have found such a beautiful land. Ergene-Kon was replete with natural resources. It was copious with alluring animals, perennial trees, green meadows, and various plants, which were more than enough for the survival of the small group. However, KayHan was almost consumed with the idea of revenge and was desperate to return to the empire in order to complete his mission. He had to wait for the right time to strike, and he needed a strong army in order to defeat the Tatars and reclaim the throne. With the passage of time, the progeny of Nukuz and KayHan multiplied.

KayHan soon assumed that the right moment to strike had arrived, and so he, along with the small but strong army he had raised, ventured back toward the path they had originally entered the valley from. He was old, but he was determined. He knew full well that the only thing that could stop him from reclaiming the throne was fate itself. Unfortunately for him, fate decided to do so. The secret passageway had disappeared from sight. KayHan and his people searched day and night for the pathway, but all of their searches resulted in failure. It was clear that KayHan would not be the one to reclaim the throne. His people continued to spend their lives within the confines of the valley, but they never gave up on their search. Over time, the clans felt the need for a larger home. The rapidly growing population of the valley, both human and otherwise, required a larger space to reside in. A place where they could all easily fit in and spend their lives. No effort was spared in their attempts to find the path and leave the valley, but they were met with failure every time.

The failures, however, allowed the legend of Ergene-Kon to eventually take place. The story of a young boy that turned the fortunes of his people around and succeeded in achieving KayHan's dream. The dream to reclaim the throne of the empire and return the people of the valley to their true home. The tale of Tu-Kin the brave.

TU-KIN

400 years later:

"Tu-Kin, my brave boy, your mother loves you a lot, and you know that, right? Please get this idea of hunting out of your mind. I know how eager you are to hunt, but you must not forget that you are too young for it now. Your father knows very well when you will be ready for it and he will take you along when the time comes."

Umay, Tu-Kin's mother, was ruffling her son's hair as she said this. She understood his want to hunt, but she was worried something would happen to him if he did so. Tu-kin, however, was not satisfied with her answer. He had an irresistible energy that he believed could only be satisfied through hunting.

"But he knows that I love hunting," Tu-Kin stated, gently pushing his mother's hand off his head, "Yet he never takes me along, even when there is someone missing from the group."

He stood up and started walking up and down the tent they were in.

"There is something about hunting that intrigues me," He explained, "I want to ride through these forests on my horse and become the greatest hunter to ever step foot in the valley. That is my dream, mother, and you know it."

Umay had almost given up on making him understand. His two

year-old sister, lying in her mother's lap, was attentively listening to every word he said as she sucked on her fingers. Her eyes widened as Tu-Kin approached her.

"Aybike, why do not you tell her something?. Tell her I want to go." Tu-Kin said as he tickled his younger sister, who chuckled in response.

Umay took a hold of her son's hands, her warmth engulfing his palms as she looked him in the eye.

"Tu-Kin, my boy, you know what we are going through already. Your father is the chief of the tribe. He has a lot of responsibilities on his shoulders, and one day, you will be his successor. This impatience does not suit a warrior like you. You are a brave boy, and you are extraordinarily gifted, but a true knight is not only a strong warrior. A true knight keeps himself humble and strikes only when the situation demands it. He is the epitome of bravery, patience, and good behaviour. You have all of those talents, but they need a little refinement. Be a little patient, my boy. You will need it. Everything happens as Tengri demands it. Your time to hunt will come soon."

Tu-Kin listened quietly, seeing his mother's eyes full of care and worry. Despite his want to hunt, Tu-Kin knew his mother was telling the truth. He had been taught of the power the sky god, Tengri, held, and if he had decided that he had to be patient, then he had no choice but to listen. Acknowledging his mother's words, Tu-Kin stepped outside the tent. Umay watched him leave and took a deep breath.

Tu-Kin was a young boy and a direct descendent of KayHan. His father, Borge-Han, was the chief of his clan and so was over-burdened as leader with the responsibility of looking after the entirety of Ergene-Kon's people. This also included leading regular searches for the passage that would help them get out of the valley, exhausting him to a great extent. This all meant he had significantly limited time to devote to his family. Despite this, he made sure to leave as much time as he had to spend with his wife and children. He was aware of his son's potential to be a powerful warrior, and also knew that in order for that potential to be realised, he would have to allow his son to go hunting in the future. The same headstrong determination that Borge-Han possessed was also seen within Tu-Kin, and, considering their lineage, this came as no surprise to the chief of the valley.

Tu-Kin was tall and square-shouldered, his brown hair contrasting greatly with his bright blue eyes. He had been born with a sacred birthmark on his right shoulder, which the elders of the valley saw as a sign that he was destined to be a powerful leader. Though this was clear to the elders, they were unsure of exactly what the future held for Tu-Kin. They had warned Borge-Han of the dangers that surrounded someone with as much expectations as Tu-Kin. As the young boy grew up, signs of his greatness began to reveal themselves. Residents of the valley would label him Tu-Kin the brave, due to both his courage and his want to aid those around him.

After the conversation with his mother, Tu-Kin went to meet his friends at their particular meeting spot, beside a towering tree within a large, open field. Ever since childhood, he had been strong friends with Artuk and Teoman. Though they all had different personalities, they always enjoyed one another's company, and their shared interest in hunting also strengthened their bond. Artuk was the joker of the group, constantly looking for pranks to play on those unsuspecting of him. Most were wary of his talent in trickery, though they would always have a good laugh over his jokes, unless they were the punch line. On the other hand, Teoman was comparatively laid-back and reserved. He was known for being calm and level-headed, as well as respectful and kind.

As Tu-Kin approached the two of them beside the tree, he could see an evil smile spread across Artuk's face. The trickster was clearly failing to hide his thoughts as he sat atop the highest branch of the tree.

Tu-Kin could tell his friend had something up his sleeve, but, as always, he was unaware of what it was. Nevertheless, he smiled at his friends and waved at them.

"It is good to see the two of you looking so happy." Tu-Kin greeted.

"It could have been very different." Teoman stated.

"What do you mean?"

"Well someone," Teoman said, motioning toward Artuk, "Decided it was a good idea to play a prank on some of the girls in the valley centre."

"Well that is no surprise."

"But then he blamed it on me."

"Oh."

The two of them looked up at Artuk, who had now started laughing out loud, almost falling off of the branch as he did so.

"You should have seen the look on his face," He chuckled, "He was almost frightened to death."

"Of course I was, I almost got beaten up." Teoman snapped back.

"You could have just fought back."

"I am not hitting a girl."

"Okay, okay, let's move on." Tu-Kin interjected, wishing for the argument to stop.

"All right then," Artuk replied, "How did your talk about hunting go?"

Tu-Kin let out a small sigh of frustration.

"I just do not understand when we will get our chance of going hunting. My parents still think I am a little child who needs to be nagged and told what to do," He said, "I mean, look at us. We are essentially adults now, but no one can see that for some reason."

"I am sure the time will come soon," Teoman said in comfort, "They are probably just worried."

"I understand, but there is no need for them to worry. I am completely capable of looking after myself."

Not knowing how to respond, Teoman remained silent, which allowed Artuk to speak up.

"Do not worry my friend, I can lift your spirits."

"How?"

"Just come over here for a second."

Curious as to what Artuk was alluding to, Tu-Kin stepped toward the tree. He soon, however, felt something wrap around his feet. In a flash, he was pulled upward into the air, finding himself looking down at the ground where Teoman was trying his best to hold in his laughter. Artuk, however, was making no effort to hold in his, and he once again started chuckling.

"Artuk!!!"

Tu-Kin was furious, more so at himself for walking into Artuk's trap when it was so obvious that he had something planned. He lifted his head up to see Artuk looking down at him with a grin.

"I cannot believe you fell for it!" He snickered.

Artuk's words were doing little to lift Tu-Kin's mood, as he had previously promised, and his constant laughter was not helping matters either. Tu-Kin yelled back in fury.

"Get me out of this now!"

He was unable to get a good look at himself, but Tu-Kin was sure he looked ridiculous hanging from his feet. He could tell his cheeks were turning red with embarrassment. Artuk eventually got down from the tree and, along with Teoman, helped him in getting out of the trap, the both of them laughing as they did so. No sooner had Tu-Kin been untangled when he started to run after Artuk, his anger wanting to get back at his friend for catching him out. Artuk, however, was too quick for him, and the prankster quickly scampered up the tree and back to the branch he had been sitting on before, a place that Tu-Kin was not bothered enough to follow him.

Teoman soon calmed Tu-Kin down enough for him to join in with the laughter, ensuring that there were no hard feelings between him and Artuk.

"Do not do that ever again." Tu-Kin ordered, "I am warning you."

"I swear I will never again even think of doing that to you." Artuk replied, though Tu-Kin could tell he was lying.

Wishing to change the subject, Tu-Kin returned the focus of their talk back to hunting.

"Do any of you have an idea of what I can do? At this rate my parents will never allow me to hunt."

His two friends could see the sadness in Tu-Kin as he let out another sigh of frustration. Believing he had an alternative, Artuk stepped in front of him.

"You know what?" He announced, "I have a way to get you into one of the hunting groups."

"And what is that?" Tu-Kin replied, his spirits lifting.

"All we need to do is secretly knock out one of the members and disguise you as him." Artuk explained, "It will not be very difficult for an expert like me. You can trust me in this regard."

He made a proud face as he boasted about his plan, but Tu-Kin wished to go hunting on merit, not by underhanded tactics. Knowing his friend was feeling this, Teoman shoved Artuk out of the way and tried his best to console his friend.

"Tu-Kin, your father is the leader of Ergene-Kon and his role means he is burdened with a lot of responsibilities. It makes sense as to why he feels overprotective of you. That is probably the only reason he hasn't allowed you to go hunting yet. But, I have an idea."

"You mean one that actually makes sense, unlike Artuk's?"

"Of course," Teoman said, "The tournament of champions is taking place soon, is it not? That is the best way to show that you have the skills necessary to survive and thrive when hunting. I believe in you, and I am sure Artuk does as well. If you train hard enough, you can easily be this year's victor and lift the chalice of champions. Seeing this, your father will have no choice but to let you go hunting."

Tu-Kin could feel butterflies within his stomach upon hearing his suggestion. The tournament of champions was the event he most looked forward to watching every year. A competition specifically designed for young warriors within the valley to showcase their talent in the field of battle. He was definitely old enough to participate this year, and there was no better way of proving his ability to everyone, especially his father.

"That is perfect!" He exclaimed in delight, "Thank you Teoman!"

Artuk, feeling a little ignored, inserted himself back into the conversation

"That is a really good suggestion, but you always have my offer Tu-Kin. If you choose my idea, you will not have to do a single thing to be allowed in."

Tu-Kin was unsure as to whether or not Artuk was being serious, but he laughed nonetheless. What he was sure about, however, was that winning the tournament of champions was his path to approval.

THE FIRST SHOT

As the progeny of KayHan and Nukuz multiplied over time, so did the disputes among them. The population of Ergene-Kon was divided into various clans that had certain social conflicts and disagreements with one another. However, they were all still united in terms of their one major issue. They agreed in thinking that the rapidly growing population was a great threat because of the small Ergene-Kon valley. They needed to find some way out of it for their survival. Every clan had its elected chief, with Tu-Kin's father, Borge-Han, the chief of the KayHan clan. As KayHan had been son of İl-Han, his clan's leader was seen as the head of the entire valley, and so, when it came to decisions regarding every clan, Borge-Han was the one who made the final say.

The people of Ergene-Kon had faith in Tengrism, the predominantly polytheistic religion that was based on shamanistic concepts of animism. They believed in the sky god Tengri as their chief deity, and worshipped him. Among other supernatural beings, they also had faith in Asena, a wolf-like creature that the residents of the valley also believed in. Asena was considered a divine being, and thus, wolves were seen as sacred animals. The residents of the valley would remember both Tengri and Asena in their prayers and religious meetings. Tu-Kin's clan was respected as one of the two most revered clans in Ergene-Kon. The other being the Nukuz clan, which was led by Dumrul-Han. As the two of them were so highly respected among their peers, the KayHan clan and the Nukuz clan had a strong rivalry.

Every year, the people of Ergene-Kon held an extensive celebration in order to show their utmost gratitude to their god, Tengri. The festivities always took place on the same day their ancestors escaped the Tatars and were blessed with the founding of Ergene-Kon. Several games were held alongside the celebrations, and the most popular of them was the tournament of champions, a competition to find the strongest warrior in the valley. The tournament would crown the victor with the Chalice of Champions, and this was regarded as a great honour for clan whose representative emerged victorious. The tournament had stern rules including an age range for competitors. As he had already turned seventeen, Tu-Kin would be able to participate in this year's edition. He was completely set on partaking and so he decided to head back home so that he could share his want to participate with his parents.

Before he arrived, Borge-Han returned to the tent. His wife was waiting for him by the fire, and it was clear that she wanted to discuss something important with him.

"Is there something you want to tell me, Umay?" He questioned, "You look tense."

Umay nodded.

"Tu-Kin wanted me to ask you something on his behalf. He desperately wants to go hunting with one of the groups. He has wanted to do this ever since he first saw you bring a catch home. The idea of hunting intrigues him more than anything else. He is gifted, Borge-Han, and you know it. I know you fear putting his life at stake but you cannot hold him back for much longer. It is his destiny to become a great warrior, and allowing him to hunt is the first step to helping him reach his full potential. At the very least, take him with you when you go hunting next time. He is not a child that needs to be looked after anymore. He is a young man, and I know he is capable of keeping himself and others safe. He is talented as an archer, he is talented as a swordsman, and he is talented as a leader. He grows frustrated with your continuous refusals. I think you should give him a chance. Let him follow his dreams. His birthmark is a blessing, but by doing this, we are treating it as a threat."

Borge-Han listened to his wife thoroughly, realizing that she was right in thinking that way. He was reluctant to let his son loose, but he understood that Tu-Kin had earned the right to walk his own path, and if that path started by allowing him to go hunting, then Borge-Han admitted that he had to grant him permission.

As Tu-Kin arrived home, he saw his parents already waiting for him in order to start eating their supper.

"Good evening, father."

"Good evening, my boy," Borge-Han replied, gently, "How was your day?"

"It was really good. In fact, Artuk played an amusing prank on me and had me flying in the air for a short while."

Hearing this, the family laughed heartily. They were all well acquainted with Artuk and his tricks.

"That does sound like a fun time, come and join us for supper. We were just waiting for you to start."

"Sure, let me just quickly wash my hands. I will be right back."

Saying this, he went outside the tent, washed his hands from a pitcher of water, and went back to join the rest of the family for supper. His mind was constantly thinking about the most appropriate words to choose, weaving a befitting sentence to put forth his idea of participation in the competition. He loved his father, but Borge-Han's aura was enough to make anyone nervous when asking him something important.

He quickly returned to the inside of the tent. Aybike was playing around on the floor having already finished her food. Tu-Kin took his place beside his parents and started eating, but his mind was still looking for the right way to ask his father about the competition.

Out of the blue, Borge-Han spoke up.

"Finish your food quickly, Tu-Kin. You have to accompany me somewhere after supper and we must be back before midnight."

Tu-Kin was startled to hear his father break the silence so suddenly. He wanted to talk to him about the competition in front of his mother due to his lack of self-confidence. The shock caused him to freeze for a second.

"Do you hear me? What is gotten into you today?" inquired his father, questioning his son's frozen state.

Tu-Kin quickly snapped out of his trance.

"Yes father, everything is fine. I am ready to go now. I do not feel like eating anyway."

"No, first you must finish your food, and then we will leave."

Once supper had finished, Borge-Han took his bow and beckoned for Tu-Kin to follow him outside the tent. Tu-Kin was a little surprised to see him taking his bow along but he followed obediently. He was further taken aback when he saw his father venture towards the woods.

"Your mother told me that you want to join one of the hunting groups. Is that true?"

"I... I... I do, but I will not be able to without your permission. I wanted to seek your approval first." Stammered Tu-Kin, who was uncertain as to why they were going into the forest.

Tu-Kin wished his mother was still present alongside them. She would have been a great help in helping Tu-Kin get his words across. Now that he was alone with his father, however, he was struggling to speak.

"I have seen you practice archery with your friends," his father claimed, "There is no doubt that you are skilled in that department."

Saying this, he turned towards Tu-Kin, who was a few steps behind him, following him in the moonlight.

"Come closer and take this bow." he said in a firm tone.

Tu-kin did not understand at first but he then stepped forward and took a hold of Borge-Han's famous bow. Borge-Han was arguably the greatest archer the valley had ever seen, and so Tu-Kin could feel his heart skip a beat when his father touted his prowess with a bow. The bow in his hand was heavier than those that Tu-Kin normally used, but he held it tightly, not daring to drop it on the ground and risk damaging it.

"Tu-Kin, you are my only son and you are very dear to me. I wanted to tell you a few things about yourself but I wished to wait for the right time to do so."

He clasped Tu-Kin by his shoulder and looked into his eyes.

"Do you know that in hunting, the most important thing is your focus over your prey? And these are not always innocent animals. They can be vicious and dangerous. You must also be brave when you are hunting, you must control your nerves. If you become afraid of what is in front of you, then you have already lost. Always look at your opponent's eyes and show them that you are not afraid."

With that said, Borge-Han led his son into a dark part of the woods. Though his father had talked about controlling his nerves, Tu-Kin could not help but feel afraid of walking through the woods in the dark. Before long, Borge-Han signalled for him to load the bow with one of the arrows. In the pitch black of the night, the moon was the only source of visibility, its ghostly light shining upon the path ahead of Tu-Kin.

Suddenly, he jumped aside. Looking down, Tu-Kin was startled at the sight he saw. The ground was littered with scorpions, each one bearing a menacing stinging tail. Wanting to avoid getting stung, Tu-Kin began jumping to and fro, causing his father to burst into roaring laughter.

"This is just a trivial hindrance, my boy! You have to be brave."

Tu-Kin felt embarrassed to hear this, and so he resorted to kicking them away with his feet. After a short while that seemed to last forever, Tu-Kin and his father finally arrived at a place free of scorpions.

"Now, you have to keep a keen eye on what you are going to see next," Borge-Han explained, "Keep your arrow steady and shoot when you feel the time is right."

"But what do I need to shoot, and how will I see it?" Tu-Kin questioned in confusion.

"Do not worry, you will see it soon. Here it comes!"

With this, Borge-Han pointed towards something that was shining in the dark. Tu-Kin held his bow tight and tried to catch a glimpse of the creature. When he finally caught sight of the animal, however, he instantly regretted travelling into the forest. It was cobra, its eyes shining like diamonds in the darkness. Tu-Kin began to shake with fear as the cobra slithered towards him.

His father, upon seeing this, shouted at his son to bring him back to his senses.

"Tu-Kin, remember what I told you. Stay calm and do not be afraid! Focus on your target and shoot. I know it is dark but use that to your advantage."

Tu-Kin shook his head upon hearing this pep-talk and pulled himself together. Tu-kin realized that the darkness could be a great help to him, the snake's eyes clearly visible in the pitch black surroundings. The sight of the deadly snake had originally caused Tu-Kin to squirm, but now, as it slithered toward him while flickering its tongue, he felt his confidence rise. He brought the bow closer to his shoulder, closed one of his eyes tightly to focus better, gritted his teeth, and took aim, the snake now only a short distance away. As the snake raised its head in order to strike, Tu-Kin let go of his bowstring. The arrow zipped through the air and pierced the snake between its eyes. Both father and son knew the snake was now dead.

"That is my boy!" exclaimed Borge-Han with pride.

Tu-Kin took a while to register what he had done, but he was soon filled with euphoria. The snake had now become his first catch, and, though it could not be eaten, Tu-Kin was overjoyed at his success. He turned towards his father with a wide grin and laughed in ecstasy.

Tu-Kin's happiness, however, could not compare to his father's joy. Borge-Han was relieved to see his son succeed. He was sure that Tu-Kin was almost ready to face the troubles lying ahead of him. Nevertheless, he knew that a little more practice would be crucial to his journey. Just before they ended their journey back home, Tu-Kin, who was once again a few steps behind his father, came to a standstill and finally said what was on his mind, his confidence boosted by his earlier success.

"Father, I wish to participate in the upcoming tournament of champions."

Now that he had finally said what he had been thinking of for most of the day, Tu-Kin eagerly awaited his father's response. Borge-Han kept silent for a while, but then, without even facing Tu-Kin, approved Tu-Kin's wish, with a nod.

Tu-Kin had not expected such a quick and positive response, forcing him to ask again.

"You mean I can really participate?"

"Yes you can, Tu-Kin," Borge-Han reiterated, turning toward his son, "But you will need to practice hard. Remember that it is no ordinary competition. It is about the pride of the whole clan, and losing means stripping it of its honour. I would suggest taking more time to think about this decision, but if you are certain, then I will support your endeavour."

Tu-Kin was unable to believe his luck. His day had started off looking hopeless, yet it had ended with promise. He was sure that he wanted to partake in the competition. If he could gain the right training and improve his fighting ability enough, then he was certain that he could claim the chalice for his clan. If he did so, then it would not be too long before he was able to go and hunt.

CONFLICT

Tu-Kin could not sleep with the excitement of sharing the news with his friends. The next day, he got out of bed before the sun could even rise. He went to see his little sister Aybike, who had a habit of waking up early in the morning and disturbing the rest of the family's slumbers. She chuckled heartily as she saw him, crawled towards her older brother, and opened her arms, asking him to lift her. He stepped forward and lifted her onto his lap. After giving her a few throws in the air, he kissed her cheeks and began to put her down. However, she was not ready to come off his lap and insisted on being lifted again. Tu-Kin realized that he had gotten himself into a slight problem. He had no option left other than to take her along. Carrying her on his shoulders, he made his way to his friends' meeting spot. In the middle of his journey, he realized that it was too early for Artuk and Teoman to appear, and that he had better head to the meadow for a morning walk. Thus he changed his route and walked towards his new destination. Aybike was continuously plucking his hair and laughing loudly throughout.

After a few minutes of walking, Tu-Kin stopped for a rest and put his sister on the green grass, which made Aybike cry.

"Come on Aybike," Tu-Kin pleaded, "Stop crying."

Despite his pleas, his sister continued to bawl, causing Tu-Kin to pick her up once again. Though he thought his touch would allow Aybike to calm down, her crying refused to stop.

"What is it with babies and crying?" Tu-Kin asked himself as he put Aybike down again.

As Aybike's tears trickled down her cheeks, Tu-Kin tried his best to think of a way to stop her cries. He ultimately decided on something he wished he did not need to do.

"Hey Aybike," Tu-Kin called, "Look at me."

With his sister's eyes on him, Tu-Kin began to jump up and down, waving his arms around and making weird noises. He thought that making himself look funny would calm Aybike down, but her distress showed no signs of stopping. Realising his action had failed, Tu-Kin hoped that no one had seen him do so. His hopes were soon dashed as he heard laughter from behind him. Turning around, his eyes lay upon a figure of beauty.

It was Buke, the daughter of Dumrul-Han, chief of Nukuz's clan. Though she was from a different clan, Tu-Kin had seen her around the valley beforehand. She was said to be one of the smartest people in the valley, specifically in the field of astronomy, as well as a kind and caring soul. She was holding some parchment papers in her hand when   Tu-Kin, who had been taken aback by her sudden appearance saw her. His face turned red at the thought of someone seeing him acting like a fool.

"You look like you need some help," Buke said, stepping forward with a smile, "May I try?"

Tu-Kin failed to come up with something to say, but quickly nodded in approval. With permission granted, Buke approached Aybike, who was still sobbing, and smiled kindly at her while placing her papers on the grass. Her hands now free, she carefully picked Aybike up and cradled her in her arms. Fortunately, Aybike did not resist Buke's approach and was soon subject to Buke singing a lullaby. Her soft voice swept gently into the baby's ears, succeeding in stopping her cries, before putting her to sleep. Tu-Kin watched on in amazement. Though he was annoyed at Aybike for not listening to him, he was stunned by the Buke's ability to calm his sister down so easily. She brought Aybike back to Tu-Kin, who retrieved his sister.

"I... I tried to make her stop," he explained, "But I was not able to."

Buke smiled, "Babies are tricky, do not be too hard on yourself."

A moment passed of the two watching Aybike sleep in her brother's arms before Buke spoke up again.

"I have heard that you will participate for your clan in the combat games this year."

Tu-Kin was shocked by the question. He had not told anyone about his participation yet, and so questioned how Buke already knew of it.

"How do you know that?" He asked in confusion.

"Your friend, Artuk, announced your participation in the centre of the valley," Buke explained, "He told everyone about your superior strength and intelligence."

"Really?"

"Yes, I was not present, but my brother, Mete, was, and he told me about it."

Mete was the son of Dumrul-Han and the pride of his clan. Dumrul-Han and Mete were both immensely powerful as well as highly arrogant. Mete had been the victor of the competition for the last decade. His constant success had led him to believe that he was invincible. He had defeated everyone in the previous year's tournament with ease, reinforcing the claim that he was the strongest warrior in the entire valley. What Tu-Kin could not believe, however, was that Mete was Buke's sibling.

"Mete is your brother?"

"Yes he is." Buke replied.

"I did not know that."

"That is a surprise, I thought we looked the same." Buke said sarcastically, causing Tu-Kin to smile and relax a little from the news.

"You do not have a problem with everyone knowing, do you?"

Buke asked.

"No, of course not, it is alright," Tu-Kin lied, "After all, everybody had to know about this sooner or later."

It was definitely not alright for Tu-Kin in actuality, he was mad at Artuk for telling everyone and was trying to come up with a way to get back at his friend.

"I think it is about time I left," Buke announced, "My father is expecting to meet me soon."

She waved goodbye and walked off into the distance as Tu-Kin continued to look at her until she was out of sight.

As she faded from view, Tu-Kin began his own walk home, making sure not to wake Aybike up from her sleep. He was adamant that Artuk had to pay for not keeping his mouth shut.

Tu-Kin soon arrived at his home in order to drop Aybike off. After refusing his mother's offer of food, he made his way over to the spot where he knew his friends were waiting for his presence. On arrival, however, he could tell that something was very wrong.

"Tu-Kin!" Teoman called, "Come here quickly."

Tu-Kin's heart raced as he ran over to his friends. Artuk lay still on the ground as Teoman kneeled beside him, beckoning Tu-Kin to quicken his pace. As he neared his friends, Tu-Kin finally saw what was wrong.

Artuk was covered with bruises, his left eye blackened, and his right arm bent at an unnatural position. He was awake, but it was clear that he had been attacked, and hurt, badly.

"What happened?!" Tu-Kin asked in fear.

"It was Mete." Teoman answered as Artuk moaned in pain beside them.

"What?!"

"I will tell you later," Teoman promised, "We need to find help for Artuk now!"

The next hour flashed by Tu-Kin in a blur. He had managed to run over to his village and get the attention of some of the healers, as well as his father and Artuk's parents. He had led all of them over to Artuk's damaged body, the sight shocking and scaring the onlookers. Though Artuk was carried off to safety, the concern for his well-being remained high as Teoman explained to everyone what had transpired.

"This is a bad idea," Teoman stated as he and Artuk approached the centre of the valley, "Tu-Kin would not want us to do this."

"You worry too much," Artuk responded, "This will improve his reputation among the clans, trust me."

Despite his friend's reassurance, Teoman still felt uneasy about what Artuk was about to do.

"This looks like a good spot." Artuk claimed, stepping atop a rock that allowed him to tower over most of the residents in the area.

With a quick cough to clear his throat, Artuk began his announcement.

"Attention everyone!"

His opening statement caused every figure in the nearby area to turn their attention toward him.

"This is a message from the KayHan clan surrounding the tournament for the chalice of champions!"

As Artuk continued his speech, Teoman could see the number of onlookers increase with each passing word.

"Our glorious clan have chosen Tu-Kin, son of Borge-Han, to represent us in the upcoming competition."

The announcement caused a good deal of gasps and commotion from within the crowd.

"I am here today to warn any fellow competitors who may be

listening to me of the unmatched strength and unrivalled intelligence that Tu-Kin possesses. If anyone of you are to encounter him in the tournament, then you will know that defeat is at your doorstep. He may be a kind and caring soul outside of the arena, but he becomes a beast when within it. All of his opponents have no choice but to beg for mercy at his feet, or else they will face his wrath."

Though Artuk continued his speech, Teoman lost his friend's trail of words when he saw a face he wished he had not in the crowd. It was Mete, and he looked angry.

"Artuk, Artuk!" Teoman said to his friend, trying to get his attention, "We have to go."

His friend continued his speech, which was now causing a lot of listeners to grow restless, some of them even yelling back at Artuk. Knowing that a fight may break out if Artuk continued, Teoman pulled him off of the rock and dragged him away from the crowd, causing them to disperse.

"So how did I sound?" Artuk asked as the two walked off.

"Annoying," Teoman responded, "Now you are going to have to explain yourself to Tu-Kin."

"Relax, it is not as if I am going to get beaten up when he finds out."

The two made their way to the tree that marked the trio's meeting place. Tu-Kin had not arrived yet, but both of them knew he would appear soon.

"I still do not understand why you had to tell everyone." Teoman admitted.

"Why not?" Artuk questioned, "I have done Tu-Kin a great deal of help, I have taken everyone off-guard, I have improved his reputation, I have..."

Artuk continued to list off the things that his speech had done to supposedly help his best friend, but Teoman soon lost interest, turning around to look across the horizon. The sun shone brightly across the grass, with a small breeze causing the blades to sway slowly. Though the view was pleasing, it was soon ruined, and it caused Teoman's stomach to churn. Mete had appeared in the distance, and he was not alone.

Teoman gulped as he turned away from Mete, hoping for the warrior and his companions to simply walk past or away from him and Artuk, who was still speaking.

"Hey you!"

The shout caused Artuk to stop his list, as the two friends turned to face the direction of the sound.

Mete stood tall as he approached the two, his companions ensuring to remain behind him as they walked. His dark brown hair drooped over his eyes, which were strained and filled with anger.

"Do not do anything stupid." Teoman whispered to his friend, who was also aware of Mete's strength.

"You were the one who announced Tu-Kin's participation, were you not?" Mete asked Artuk as he stood a few paces ahead of the two.

"Guilty as charged." Artuk admitted, smiling.

Mete let out a burst of laughter.

"I thought your clan was smarter than to allow their heir to take part in something he has no chance of winning."

His statement caused his companions to chuckle as well, but it also made Artuk step forward.

"How are you so sure?" He asked.

"Is it not obvious," Mete replied, "He is small, he is thin and he is weak. My clan has toddlers the same height as he is, not only that, but they have more muscle on them. I doubt Tu-Kin could beat my grandmother in a fight."

He and his companions continued to laugh until Artuk replied.

"Oh is that so, hunchback?"

The laughter quickly faded.

"What did you just call me?"

Teoman could see Artuk grinning, making him realise that his friend was about to ignore his earlier statement.

"You heard me, you baboon, how can you expect to defeat Tu-Kin with a stomach as round as yours. You believe he is small, thin and weak, but you are quite clearly fat, slow and dumb. I am sure your current undefeated record has caused your ego to grow to the same size as your belly, but I can assure you that you have only been winning all this time because your opponents have been subject to your breath. You must eat your father's excrement for dinner to have a stench that bad. I have seen hounds with much less hair on their body than you, and they also had much cleaner teeth. Do you even know what a chew stick is?"

Artuk's insults had clearly made Mete mad, his face had turned red with anger and he was breathing far heavier.

"You have ten seconds to get out of here before I break every bone in your body." He uttered with malicious intent.

"Ten seconds? I could give you an entire day to do the same thing but I am not so sure you would be able to make it far in that time. Why the red face? Are you upset that you continue to lose to slugs in foot races? I would not be worried if I were you, your heavy breathing makes me think you would pass out from the effort, so it would be best if you stopped racing them. Why not try another hobby, such as learning some mathematics? I will gladly teach you what a number is if you ask."

Artuk's disregard for Mete's anger pushed the warrior over the edge. Teoman caught a glimpse of Mete raising his fist, but he was unable to stop the inevitable. The fist struck Artuk across the face, causing him to sprawl onto the floor. Before Teoman could react, Mete's companions had grabbed him and pulled him away. They were not attacking him, but they were stopping him from helping his friend. Teoman tried his hardest to break free of their holds, but he could do nothing but watch his friend get attacked by Mete.

Each punch, whether to Artuk's face or his stomach, was filled with pure rage as Mete showed no mercy. Though Mete knew Artuk was no match for him in a fight, he ensured that Artuk would pay for his insults. After a few minutes of violent attacks, Mete signalled to some of his friends for help.

"Get that rock over there!" He yelled.

The cronies quickly brought the rock, which was jagged and large, over to Mete, who placed the rock underneath Artuk's elbow.

"Hold his arm."

Mete's friends held Artuk's arm outstretched over the rock, making it clear what Mete had in mind. Teoman wanted to shout, but he knew no amount of pleading would stop Mete's attack.

"Do not you ever disrespect me ever again!" Mete yelled, lifting his foot up and thrusting it down upon Artuk's forearm.

The snap was deafening. Though Teoman had shut his eyes as Mete's foot came down, he opened them to see Artuk's arm bending in the complete opposite direction to what was natural. His arm was broken, and his screams proved the pain he was in.

Having broken Artuk's arm, Mete grinned at the destruction he had caused and turned around, walking back the way he came.

Those who had held Teoman back quickly shoved him against the tree, before one of them struck him in the stomach. The blow caused Teoman to drop to his knees in pain, but he knew he was suffering far less than his friend. He slowly crawled over to Artuk, who was still moaning in pain as Mete and his gang disappeared into the distance. He needed help, and fast.

"And that is what happened." Teoman finished off, having told everyone what had happened.

The listeners all listened on horrified as Teoman had explained what Mete had done to Artuk, who had been carried home and was currently being treated by a healer beside the group. Though his parents wished to aid in his treatment, they also wanted to know the reason behind the attack. Now that they did, they were both furious.

"This is unacceptable," Artuk's father stated in anger, "Mete must face consequences for this."

"I am afraid we are unable to do anything for now." Borge-Han admitted.

"Why not?" Artuk's mother asked in frustration, "He should be punished for what he has done."

"What he did was horrible, but he is the son of Dumrul-Han," Borge-Han stated, "If we were to do the same to him, we would create outrage across the valley."

Though Artuk's parents were angered at their son's attack, they knew Borge-Han was right. A war between clans would cause nothing but pain and destruction to the valley. There was a moment of silence before it was broken.

"I will do it."

Everyone turned to Tu-Kin, who had spoken.

"I will defeat Mete in the tournament. Anything is allowed in the arena, right? I will win the chalice for our clan, I will get revenge for Artuk and the Nukuz clan will not be able to do anything about it."

Though Tu-Kin was mad at Artuk's announcement his feelings had been replaced by concern and worry for his friend after he realized what had happened. His anger was now directed solely at Mete.

Artuk's parents took a moment to register Tu-Kin's statement before Artuk's mother went over to him and hugged him.

"Do our son proud," she pleaded, "Win the tournament for us and the clan."

"I will." Tu-Kin promised as she let go.

"We will stay with Artuk now, may Tengri keep you safe."

Tu-Kin and his father left the tent, allowing Artuk's parents to stay with their son while he recuperated from the attack. As they left, Borge-Han approached Tu-Kin.

"My son," He said, laying a hand on his shoulder, "I know someone who can train you for the tournament."

"Really?"

"Yes, but I warn you, you must not train or fight in anger. I know that you want to hurt Mete, but if you lose your head you will also lose the fight."

"I understand father."

"I will take you to Bayhan, one of my closest friends, I am sure that he will be able to improve your physical capacities."

Tu-Kin was relieved that someone had been found for him to train under. Though his father had warned him, he still wanted Mete to pay for what he had done to Artuk.

"Be wary though," His father continued, "Bayhan is a strict perfectionist, always do as he says and make sure you perform every task he throws at you to the best of your ability."

"I will."

The day had gotten dark for Tu-Kin, but the knowledge that his father had found a trainer for him improved his spirits. If Bayhan really was as good a trainer as his father had claimed he was, than Tu-Kin was sure that he could defeat Mete and win the tournament for both Artuk and his clan.

THE PRACTICE
BEGINS

Not only was Bayhan one of Borge-Han's strongest subordinates, he also used to go hunting with Tu-Kin's father regularly. A big reason for choosing him for the training was his commendable expertise in the art of fighting. He was a few years older than Borge-Han, and so, he was relatively old, but his skills and knowledge remained second-to-none. He had a slim build and sported a beard of grey, bushy hair around his mouth. Tu-Kin found it hard to tell that he had been one of the strongest warriors of his time as he stood in front of his new trainer. Borge-Han had taken Tu-Kin to the field soon after breakfast, safe in the knowledge that his friend would be there. No sooner had they arrived when Bayhan encountered them, giving his friend a tight hug. After an exchange of greetings, Bayhan glared at Tu-Kin, as if trying to analyse the strengths and capabilities that the young man possessed. After a moment of doing so, Bayhan invited the two to his camp.

In the camp, Bayhan took no time in serving his two guests some of Ergene-Kon's renowned, special tea.

"It has been such a long time since I have had this tea," Borge-Han exclaimed with a tone of nostalgia, "It reminds me of the days when we would hunt together."

Bayhan smiled at the thought.

"I still remember having to be the one to catch our prey because you were too slow, never forget that you would have been hopeless without me."

The two laughed at the memories as they drank. Tu-Kin, however, was not interested in tales of their friendship. His mind was being overflowed by questions as to how the old, thin man was going to help him win the competition.

It was not too long before Borge-Han spoke again.

"Bayhan, my son will take part in this year's combat games, and I want you to train him. You are the only man I could trust in this regard. You are free to choose whatever training methods you wish. I want him to be as tough as you by the end of it. In fact, even better than you, and I know I can trust you with this."

It took Bayhan a short moment for him to understand what his friend had asked of him.

"I understand. So this is what brought you here....."

After a short pause and a few deep breaths, he continued.

"I suppose you have already told your son about how I am. He will have to have an iron will and a great amount of determination."

"Yes, that goes without saying. Everything is up to you, you may do as you see fit."

Drinking his last drops of tea, Bayhan turned to Tu-Kin.

"You can come from tomorrow," he announced, "But only before the sun can see you coming."

Tu-Kin was puzzled by his last words.

"What do you mean by that?"

Bayhan chuckled at Tu-Kin's surprise.

"I mean arrive here before sunrise of course."

Though Tu-Kin was still mystified by the comment, he knew it would be unwise of him to refuse the offer.

Just before the two guests left, Borge-Han placed his hand on Bayhan's shoulder.

"Train him hard, Bayhan, for the coming days. For the threats of which you know. I entrust him to you."

Bayhan nodded in response. Tu-Kin was unable to understand what his father meant, and began to grow curious.

The next morning, Tu-Kin ate his breakfast in a hurry and travelled toward the appointed spot. However, the sun had already started spreading its beams over the land, the birds of the valley had begun chirping, and Tu-Kin did not realize that he was late for his first day of training. He did not know exactly what to expect either, causing his excitement to simmer. As he arrived, he saw Bayhan standing on one of his legs, with his eyes closed and his hands clasped in a strange manner. Tu-Kin tried to get near Bayhan without making any noise. He wanted to get a closer look at him, but as he neared the old man, Bayhan, without even opening his eyes, spoke up.

"Late for the very first day, I see."

The words startled Tu-Kin.

"Stand on that cliff." Bayhan ordered loudly.

Tu-Kin already felt bad for arriving late, and so he followed Bayhan's orders without hesitation as to avoid angering his new trainer.

A strong breeze swept through Tu-Kin's hair as he carefully made his way to the tip of the cliff. It was situated near a beautiful waterfall, one that Ergene-Kon was blessed to host, though it was also evidently dangerous. The waterfall would constantly splash against the rocks as it gushed down, and it was clear that the cliff Tu-Kin was currently standing on had sustained a lot of these splashes, its slippery surface causing Tu-Kin to ensure his footing was secure.

"Take your shirt off."

"What?"

The order shocked Tu-Kin. Taking his shirt off would force him to bear the full brunt of the winds that shot over the cliff.

"No, I know you heard me correctly. Take your shirt off."

Tu-Kin looked over to see that Bayhan had still not moved from his initial position, his eyes were still shut and his hands remained clasped. He was perplexed at the trainer's orders.

"Now!!!" Bayhan roared, knowing full well that Tu-Kin had yet to listen to his instruction.

Tu-Kin made sure to take his shirt off after that.

The winds had instantly caused him to shiver and he was worried that he would catch a cold if he continued to leave his skin unprotected against the ice-like breeze.

Bayhan turned towards his trainee before ordering him to run five laps around the area. Tu-Kin began to walk, but the cold was stopping him from increasing his speed. He had only taken a few steps before he heard a loud whistle from behind him. It was obvious that Bayhan had made the noise, but it was unclear as to why. The uncertainty was soon solved.

A dark blur shot out of Bayhan's camp, the shadow bearing down on Tu-Kin. As it raced toward him, he could just about make out its bright, yellow eyes and large, knife-like teeth. The sight caused Tu-Kin's body to wake up, and started sprinting, his feet pounding the ground as his arms swung wildly in the air. The creature continued to chase him around the area, showing no signs of slowing down or losing interest, ensuring that Tu-Kin continued to run.

The sheer panic that Tu-Kin felt at the sight of the animal made it a pleasant surprise when Bayhan whistled once more, causing his pursuer to stop and walk on over to the trainer.

"That is five laps."

Now that he could focus and slow down, Tu-Kin could see that the chaser was a strongly-built hound, its eyes and teeth being no different from what Tu-Kin thought he had seen. As his heart punched the inside of his chest, he was relieved that he had not been caught by the hound, which was now getting its neck scratched by Bayhan.

"Good boy." Bayhan said in affection as the hound licked his hand.

After the neck scratch, both Bayhan and the hound walked over to Tu-Kin, who was still trying his best to get his breath back.

"Do you feel cold anymore?" The trainer asked with a hint of sarcasm.

Though Tu-Kin was tired, Bayhan was right, his body had warmed up considerably. He looked over at Bayhan, who had a smile plastered on his face, and then at the hound, who had its tongue out as evidence of its exhaustion.

"Tu-kin, you have unlimited powers inside you, and they need to be tamed. You must learn how to control them before they control you. I have heard you are good at archery. Take your time, and then get up."

Bayhan then placed the end of his stick on Tu-Kin's shoulders, specifically on his birthmark, before taking a few steps back. Tu-Kin was still panting. His trainer's words made him believe that he had plenty of time to catch his breath, but that was soon proven wrong.

"Get up! On your feet! Hurry!"

Tu-Kin did not want to get up but he had already faced the consequences of his reluctance before. Wanting to avoid getting into more trouble, he stood up as straight as he could.

"We have to move to that place." Bayhan stated as he pointed at another cliff that was even closer to the waterfall.

At that point, Tu-Kin questioned whether the man was trying to train him or kill him. Regardless, he knew he had to listen to

Bayhan's orders. As they reached the second cliff, Bayhan pointed towards a tall tree that towered over the two.

"Climb this tree, and as you reach the top, let me know so I can tell you where to jump."

With that said, he moved back into his initial pose as the hound continued to stare at Tu-Kin, who was perplexed. He contemplated refusing the order before being interrupted by the hound once again. Reluctantly, he climbed up the tree in order to avoid being bitten.

As he reached the top, Bayhan opened his eyes and lifted his arm, pointing.

"Jump there!"

Tu-Kin turned to look at the required landing zone and felt his stomach drop. He had no idea as to how he could survive the fall that was being requested of him. Looking back at Bayhan, Tu-Kin could tell that his trainer would not have a change of mind. After taking a moment to register the jump once again, Tu-Kin had no choice but to prepare himself, and jump.

"Please save me, Tengri."

There was split second of nothingness before Tu-Kin felt himself crash against the ground. He took the entire force of the landing on the side of his chest, as well as his right arm and leg. The pain took no time in invading Tu-Kin's nerve system, causing him to let out a gasp of agony.

Rolling onto his back, Tu-Kin opened his eyes to see Bayhan and the hound looking over him.

"You okay?" asked Bayhan as the hound licked its lips.

"I just fell about twenty feet from the top of a tree and landed on my ribcage, how can I be okay?"

Bayhan roared with laughter.

"Do not be a chicken," he teased, "Look, in order to be strong and to face people like Mete, you must exit your comfort zone. Things will not always go the way you please."

"You got that right."

"Oh come on, boy, that was an easy task."

"It did break my ribcage but I guess you are right." Tu-Kin responded sarcastically while using his remaining strength to get to his feet.

The rest of the training session was filled with practices that Tu-Kin found far easier to bear than the two he had been initially assigned. At the conclusion of the session, Bayhan told Tu-Kin to put his shirt back on. It was the toughest day of Tu-Kin's life, but he also knew that it was only the first day of many. Before he could leave, Bayhan called him over. As he approached his trainer, Tu-Kin was caught out by Bayhan's stick, which struck his abdomen with force.

"Do not come late tomorrow."

Tu-Kin noted that he would have to get up early the next morning.

It was still noon when Tu-Kin arrived back home, taking the opportunity to have a warm bath and a peaceful rest. Though Borge-Han had seen the bruises on his son's body, he chose not to question it.

That evening, Tu-Kin shared the details of the session with Teoman, who was intrigued by Bayhan's training methods.

"I am surprised you did not get seriously hurt."

"Same here," Tu-Kin responded, "But I know that what he is doing is for the best. If my father believes in him then I should too."

Though the day had been tough on him, Tu-Kin had not forgotten about Artuk.

"How is he?" He asked Teoman, who had spent time with Artuk during Tu-Kin's training.

"He has still been making jokes and smiling," Teoman responded, "But his arm needs to heal and the bruises remain on his face."

"You mean he is still smiling despite what happened to him?"

"Of course he is, but do not get it wrong, he still wants revenge on Mete."

Whether Artuk had wanted to get back at his attacker or not, Tu-Kin had made defeating Mete his number one priority in the competition. Though he wanted to win the entire tournament, he would still be happy going home empty handed if it meant embarrassing the heir of the Nukuz clan in front of the entire valley.

"I will visit him tomorrow after training," Tu-Kin explained to Teoman, "I will tell him myself that I will defeat Mete for him."

The next day Tu-Kin arrived at the cliff in time to avoid another sharp blow of the thin stick. The day started identically to the last. No sooner had he reached the scene and taken off his shirt when the hound started running after him again. The task had been made even harder because of an increase in laps, Bayhan having ordered Tu-Kin to run two more. Once the laps had been completed, the hound returned to its owner, who approached Tu-Kin.

"Now then," The trainer explained as Tu-Kin recovered from the run, "For today's session I have enlisted a friend of yours to help us."

Tu-Kin was taken aback by the statement, and his shock was compounded as he saw Teoman appear from behind Bayhan.

"Teoman?"

His friend waved at him in a friendly manner.

"Teoman here has asked me to help him in improving his strength as well, he wants to become stronger."

Tu-Kin had been unaware of his friend's want to train, but thinking of it now, he understood why Teoman wanted to join in his training.

"I cannot let myself be stopped from saving a friend again," He explained, "I want to be able to make a difference from now on."

"Both of you have understandable reasons for wanting to train," Bayhan stated, "So let us start today's work."

"What do you want us to do?" Tu-Kin asked in eagerness.

"To begin, stand an arm's width in front of one another."

The two students did as they were told.

"We will proceed with a simple exercise, you two will take turns to strike one another across the stomach. You must not weaken your shots simply because you are friends. Show me your strength and continue until one of you can take no more. This is not a competition, this is simply to see how much damage you can take. Teoman will go first."

The two friends looked at one another in apology, but they both knew that they had to do as Bayhan said unless they wanted to be kicked out of the session. The two prepared themselves for the task at hand.

"Begin."

The start of the task signalled, Tu-Kin clenched his right fist and flung it towards Teoman's lower stomach. The impact stung Tu-Kin's fingers but it was evident that Teoman was also hurt as he stumbled back before regaining his balance. After a few seconds to regain breath, Tu-Kin readied himself to bear the brunt of Teoman's strike. The blow pained Tu-Kin, but he took it far better than how Teoman took his punch. The activity lasted for a few more minutes before Teoman fell to his knees and admitted he had reached his limit.

With the task over, Tu-Kin also sat down. Though his stomach had held up for longer than his friend's it was still in pain, and so he took the opportunity to recuperate.

"Hmmm," Bayhan mumbled stroking his beard, "Both of you sustained more than I thought you would, but I know you can do better. Use this chance to get your breath back before we continue on to the next task."

◆ ◆ ◆

The session had taken a lot out of the two pupils by the time it had ended. Though Tu-Kin had known what to expect, his heart still tried its best to rip out of his chest at the conclusion of the final activity. Teoman was not too dissimilar. The both of them had travelled over to Artuk's house after training in order to see their friend, who was surprised to see the two of them so tired. Though some of his bruises had disappeared, his arm was still broken. As Teoman had mentioned before, however, he was still smiling and light-hearted.

"I cannot believe you joined in too," He said to Teoman, "It was about time you got some muscles."

"Ha ha," Teoman responded in sarcasm as Tu-Kin genuinely chuckled beside him, "I have more muscle than you do."

"Do not get too overconfident," Artuk warned, "If I did not have this broken arm I would have already completed your training."

"In two days?"

"Of course."

Though it was clear Artuk was lying, Tu-Kin felt relieved at being able to see his friend smile and hear him crack more jokes. Though his body still needed repair, it was clear that his spirit did not. Even so, Tu-Kin still wanted revenge for Artuk.

"Do not rush your recovery." He told Artuk.

"What do you mean?"

"I know you want to get back at Mete."

"Well, of course I do."

"Exactly, so take the time to recuperate and I will embarrass him for you, in front of the entire valley no less!"

THE TRAINING CONTINUES

Bayhan's training sessions continued, each one causing Tu-Kin and Teoman to exceed their physical limits. Though his friend never managed to perform tasks as well as he did, Tu-Kin could tell that Teoman was succeeding in his aim. There was still, however, one more important thing for Tu-Kin to train on before he could believe in his goal.

"You may be wondering where your friend is." Bayhan explained to Tu-Kin as he stood ready for his latest session.

His trainer was correct. Teoman had yet to appear at the site for the day's work, and the sun had already appeared in the sky a short while before. The reason for which was quickly stated.

"I have ordered Teoman to train alone with me in the afternoon for the time being."

"Why is that?" Tu-Kin wondered in curiosity.

"Because for these coming days we are focusing on something that centres around you and your ability with this thing. Teoman seeks to get stronger, but what you will be doing for these seven days is not what he needs."

Tu-Kin's curiosity continued until he saw Bayhan reach behind his back. With a swift pull from his arm, he revealed a long, wooden sword, not deadly but still evidently heavy.

"You will now be training with weapons," Bayhan stated, "Usage of weapons in the tournament is an essential key to victory. I have heard that you are great with weaponry, but I need to see you become excellent at it."

With that said, Bayhan threw the sword toward his pupil. Tu-Kin managed to catch the weapon before it hit the ground, though its weight threw him off balance temporarily. Though the sword was not made of metal, its carving was immaculate, each curve and edge not too dissimilar from a real sword. The handle was also thicker than the blade, proving that the sculptor performed his job well on this creation.

"You will start the day easy," Bayhan ordered, "Go to the tree and practice your sword swings on it. Ensure that your balance is not lost, and that you swing the blade at an angle that prevents air resistance from slowing your strike."

After acknowledging his trainer's order, Tu-Kin walked over to the tree. It was the same perennial plant that he had jumped off of on the first day of his training. He had a slight dislike of the tree, and so the task at hand was a good way to get back at the looming plant. Though his skill with a sword was not the best asset in Tu-Kin's arsenal, he knew that he was above average when it came to that department. His first few swings, however, did not feel right to him.

They were slow and inaccurate, each blow struck the tree at different points, and the blows themselves felt weak.

"Do not get frustrated," Bayhan said from behind him, "The sword you are using is heavier than a regular sword. If you can perfect this, then using a metal blade will be of no problem to you. Focus on catching the prefect angle for your strikes."

Despite the advice, Tu-Kin still felt uneasy as he continued to strike the tree. He knew that the weight of the wood would slow his blows, but he felt as if he was capable of doing more with the sword than what he was doing, especially after all of his physical training beforehand.

◆ ◆ ◆

"That is enough for now," Bayhan exclaimed after another half hour of the task, "You may not feel good about your sword skills now but you will by the end of this training."

Before Tu-Kin could contemplate further over his performance, Bayhan brought up a weapon that made him smile.

"It is about time I see what you can do with a bow and arrow, follow me."

Tu-Kin's morale instantly increased at the announcement of his favourite combat weapon, and so he followed his trainer with excitement. Bayhan led him to a part of the field that was vast and open, with no trees positioned within the area. Beside Tu-Kin was a bow and a quiver of arrows while in the far distance were a group of wooden boards, each at differing points. It was evident that these were targets.

"I know that you have your own personal bow," Bayhan explained, "But for this task you will use this one instead."

With that said, Bayhan motioned for his pupil to pick up the weapon. The bow was big, dwarfing the one Tu-Kin normally wielded in size, and the detail that had gone into its carving was even more impressive than that of the wooden sword.

"As this bow is larger than a normal one, it will be easier to launch the arrows over a far distance," The trainer explained, "But you will need more care on accuracy. Reaching these targets should be simple for you, but hitting them is a different story all together. For now, you will focus on that."

As Bayhan stepped away from the field, Tu-Kin sucked his finger and lifted it. The wind was not as strong as it had been in the recent days, thought there was a small breeze flying toward the north, which would aid the arrows in their flight. Confident in his ability with a bow, Tu-Kin wasted no more time in taking an arrow out of the quiver situated on the ground next to him and placing it on the bow.

Taking the wind speed and direction into consideration, Tu-Kin pulled the bowstring back as far as he thought necessary, aiming for the target closest to him. His eyes locked onto the path of flight the arrow was to take before he let go of the string, sending the arrow soaring through the air. Though his aim had seemed perfect, the arrow eventually clipped the top of the target, tumbling behind it with a clatter. He had missed.

"This bow's size is more of a factor then I thought it was." Tu-Kin said to himself as he readied another arrow.

It was clear that his pulls on the string did not need as much force as usual, though the pupil knew that adjusting to the bow would take some effort. He aimed for the same target and ensured he did not pull the string as far back as his first attempt. The arrow zipped through the air once more before successfully hitting the target, albeit to the left of the centre, a small error that annoyed the archer.

"Third time is the charm."

With another placement of arrow on bow, Tu-Kin gripped his weapon with strength. Though he had had to adjust his technique because of the size of the bow, he still had high standards for himself when it came to archery. Despite his two prior shortcomings, Tu-Kin believed the third shot would be the one to hit the bullseye. And he was correct. The arrow looped over the field as it struck through the air resistance, dipping just in time to bury its head into the centre of the wooden board.

Tu-Kin fist pumped in glee. Though he was aware of the fact he had a long way to go before he truly perfected the art of archery, he had managed to hit the bullseye with his new bow. There were still a lot of steps to take, but progress had been made.

As the competition neared, the training became tougher. The

scheduled sessions consistently caused Tu-Kin to reach his physical limit, leaving his muscles sore and his energy tank empty by the end of each one. The most important thing, however, was that Tu-Kin felt successful in every task that was ordered of him, ensuring that he left no activity incomplete. Bayhan had caused him to endure a lot of pain, but he knew of the difference the training had made. It easily proved that Tu-Kin could go above and beyond what the young man thought he was capable of. He felt as if he had unlocked an inner power.

The day before the competition, Tu-Kin arrived at the cliff to find Bayhan in his usual pose. He was, however, taken aback by his trainer's unusually calm and warm greeting.

"Good morning Tu-Kin, you look great today." Bayhan greeted with a smile, "As you will show your strength in the tournament tomorrow, I have something to ask."

"What is it?" Tu-Kin replied.

"What do you believe is the essential skill for this competition?"

Tu-Kin thought about his answer for a moment before responding.

"I reckon it is my physical strength. I feel like I have gotten a lot stronger, and so it will help me the most in the competition."

"No Tu-Kin. Though you have gotten a lot stronger, the most important powers come from within. They already lie inside you even if they are a little untamed. I have tried my best to help you control them, but there is much more to you than what meets the eye. Remember, a true hero does not solely rely on his physical powers. He believes in himself and never surrenders to what is wrong, even if it costs him his life. The competition is no ordinary event, but it is not the end of the world. I have not trained you merely for tomorrow. I have trained you for your future. You are destined to be a great warrior."

"Your powers are here," Bayhan stated, pointing at his temple, "Unleash the hero inside of you."

With that said, Bayhan walked toward his camp.

"There is no training for today. Go ahead and enjoy your time."

Tu-Kin realized that Bayhan had let him decide his own training for the final day. He went straight to a place adjacent to the woods, an area he knew he would be uninterrupted in. He took his shirt off and started practicing everything he had learned from Bayhan. Though he trained considerably, his stamina failed to significantly decrease, a far cry from the first day of training.

Curious as to see how strong he had truly become, Tu-Kin looked over at a nearby tree. Its trunk was thick and its roots snaked across the ground as if permanently attached to it. Or so it seemed. With a huge breath and a surge of strength, Tu-Kin wrapped his arms around the tree and heaved. Though it was not immediate, the tree was soon uprooted, soil dripping from the now uprooted bottom of the plant. Tu-Kin quickly tossed the tree to his side, the plant thudding against the ground and shaking the nearby area.

Tu-Kin took a few moments to regain his breath, marvelling at what he had accomplished. As he did so, he heard a gasp from behind him. Turning around in confusion, he saw Buke standing there in shock. Tu-Kin was surprised to see her.

"You?" He said in astonishment as he wasted no time in order to put his shirt back on.

Buke held her parchments with care as she explained her appearance.

"I was just passing by. Actually, I come here now and then to study. I heard a loud noise and so I came to see what happened."

"Oh, you mean this?" Tu-kin claimed, pointing at the tree as he lazily attempted to cover up his action, "This was already falling. I did not do anything."

Though Buke was not convinced, she had caught a glimpse of the mark on Tu-Kin's shoulder before he had put his shirt back on. Her knowledge of astrology had caused her to become curious.

"When did you get that mark?" She asked.

"What? The one on my shoulder? It is a birthmark."

Buke began to contemplate over something and then, after a short pause, sat down on the green grass and started looking through her parchment papers. She eventually took one out of the stack and examined it carefully. A moment later, she smiled and showed Tu-Kin the parchment's contents.

"Look, it is the same mark that you have!"

Tu-Kin took the parchment from Buke's hands and studied it. It had been drawn on several times and the depictions intrigued Tu-Kin. There was a sketch of a small fawn, coloured in gold as well as an illustration of a much bigger wolf beside it. Several pieces of information surrounded the drawings, with the fawn marked as 'sacred' and 'holy'. The wolf was labelled 'Asena'. Though Tu-Kin was unaware of the fawn, he knew about Asena, one of his people's hallowed gods. The two drawings were enticing, but Tu-Kin's focus quickly fell on the sketch at the bottom of the parchment. It near-perfectly matched his birthmark.

"It is," He said, puzzled, "Does that matter?"

"Of course it does," Buke responded in excitement, "Do you not know what that sign represents?"

"No?"

"As an astrologist, I spend my time looking at the stars for new constellations and signs. And this one is pretty much identical to your birthmark. The elders that I spoke to about this sign claimed it represents those who have hidden powers within them, powers that are unique to the mark's bearer. If that is true, then you must be destined to become a true warrior, what you did to that tree seems to prove it."

"So, you look at stars to find the destiny of people in the valley?"

"Yes."

"That makes no sense."

"Come on Tu-Kin have some faith in the stars, you cannot uproot a tree of that size and claim it was nothing special. It is a sign that what the elders have told me is true. You hold unimaginable power."

Though the thought of genuinely holding unmatched power appeased Tu-Kin, he was sure that what Buke had told him was a simple over-exaggeration of his abilities. He felt strong, but not as strong as what she was detailing. His uncertainty led him to try and end the discussion.

"I appreciate your findings," He told Buke, giving her back the paper "But I am sure this is just a simple birthmark, it should not mean anything special."

"Alright, if you do not want to talk about it, I will not continue further." Buke replied, getting back to her feet and walking off.

"The tree did look heavy," She said as she left, "You must have been practicing a lot. Good luck for the competition."

Once she had left his sight, Tu-Kin was torn between believing what Buke had told him and playing it off as crazy talk.

"I guess we will find out tomorrow." He said to himself as he left the scene.

He decided to venture back to Bayhan's camp. Tu-Kin wanted to perfect his technique with weapons before the tournament. The short journey soon passed him by as he arrived back at his trainer's tent. What stood out almost immediately, however, was that he could hear two very familiar voices in the near distance. He quickly made his way over to the field just in time to see an arrow embed itself within one of the far away wooden boards. Standing in front of him, were both Teoman and Artuk, who, miraculously, was the one with the bow in his hand.

"Artuk?" Tu-Kin said in surprise.

His two friends simultaneously turned their heads toward him.

"There he is." Teoman stated as Tu-Kin approached them.

"Where have you been?" Artuk asked.

"Never mind that," Tu-Kin stated, "How are you shooting arrows with this bow, I thought your arm was broken?"

"Not anymore," Artuk claimed with pride, "Apparently, my bones heal faster than normal and my arm is almost perfectly fixed."

"Almost?"

"Well I still feel some stings if I move it unnaturally, but other than that I am completely fine."

It had been a long while since Artuk's arm had been broken by Mete, but it was still unfathomable to Tu-Kin as to how his friend had managed to heal almost completely in that time period.

"You see?" Artuk said with a laugh, "I am stronger than you."

"Yeah right." Tu-Kin replied, joining in with the laughter.

After the laughter subsided, Tu-Kin looked over at the targets.

"I see you have been shooting some arrows."

"People do not call me the best archer in the valley for nothing." Artuk said proudly.

"Last time I checked," Teoman interjected, "No one called you that."

"I am not surprised," Tu-Kin added, "Why are there so many arrows on the ground and only one on the target if you are the best archer in the valley?"

"Okay look," Artuk tried to explain, "I was warming up."

Teoman and Tu-Kin raised their eyebrows at their friend's statement.

"Fine," Artuk stated, "How about I give you a little challenge then?"

"A challenge?"

"Yes, I challenge you to hit all of those targets, dead-centre, before I count to ten."

Teoman's eyes widened.

"That is impossible."

Tu-Kin, however, felt otherwise.

"Challenge accepted."

Artuk handed the bow over to Tu-Kin, who had certainty amazed Teoman.

"Remember, you have until the count of ten."

Tu-Kin carefully placed one of the arrows on his bow as he waited for Artuk to start the challenge. He finalized the order of targets in his mind and grinned.

"Go!"

As the word left Artuk's mouth, Tu-Kin pulled the bowstring back and let go in a flash. The arrow perfectly nestling in the centre of the first target after a piercing flight through the air. Wasting no time, Tu-Kin took another arrow and did likewise.

Each arrow struck the air with force, and each arrow buried itself in the centre of their target. The final arrow became a blur as it followed in the footsteps of those before it, hitting the centre of the wooden board.

The challenge had been beaten.

Both Artuk and Teoman stood on the spot, stunned at the speed and precision of Tu-Kin's shots. He had hit the centre on each individual strike, and had done so within the time limit.

"Challenge? What challenge?" Tu-Kin said with a beaming smile on his face, "The other competitors in the tournament will not know what hit them."

THE TOURNAMENT OF CHAMPIONS

The day finally arrived. The day where a champion would be crowned and a clan would celebrate their success. The day Tu-Kin had so eagerly anticipated from the moment his father had allowed him to participate.

The arena was filled to the brim with onlookers of all ages, each excited at the prospect of their clan's representative being crowned champion. They were all situated in stands that made them tower over the competitors, ensuring every spectator would have a good view of the tournament. Though Tu-Kin was confident in his abilities, he knew full well that every other fighter had worked just as hard as he had, and were just as strong as he was. Claiming the chalice of champions would be no easy feat.

Before the tournament commenced, the rules were announced to the crowd. The one rule that stuck out amongst the others was the one that had been on Tu-Kin's mind since he had woken up. Death was a very real possibility in the competition even though no one had met their end for several years. Tu-Kin was sure that he did not want to kill anyone, but he could not speak for his opponents.

The one fight-per-round rule was a key component to the tournament. Each fighter only had to worry about one opponent at one time. There would be no cheap shots, no sneak attacks and no cowardice. This competition was to be fought with honour and integrity.

"Are you ready?" Borge-Han asked his son as Tu-Kin strapped on his armour.

"Yes."

"I know that you are nervous, but always remember that you are my champion, no matter what."

Tu-Kin smiled at his father.

"With you, mother and Aybike in the crowd cheering me on, there is no way I can lose."

The crowd became hysteric throughout the tournament. To the relief of the fans, every fighter gave their all in their fights, each one looking to lay claim to the title of the strongest warrior in the valley. Despite this, progression through the rounds was of no difficulty to Mete. Even those who had looked set to give him a tough time were easily dealt with by the current champion, who wasted no sweat in making his way to the final.

Tu-Kin's position in the bracket had meant that if he were to face Mete, it would be in the final, and even though there were times when there were questions surrounding his ability to reach that stage, Tu-Kin managed to progress, eventually defeating a brawly warrior from another clan to set up a final showdown with the reigning champion.

The crowd noise heightened as the two finalists entered the battleground, one being the reigning champion, and the other having exceeded expectations throughout the competition. Despite the heart and ability that Tu-Kin had shown in his prior fights, most of the spectators were expecting his underdog journey to end at the hands of Mete, who had yet to be given a real challenge.

As he walked onto the battlefield, Tu-Kin made note of the weapons that littered the arena. He knew they would be pivotal in emerging victorious, but managing to reach the weapons without being stopped by Mete would be an accomplishment in itself. His eyes darted from left to right, looking for the bow and quiver of arrows, his weapon of choice. He finally caught sight of them, raising his spirits temporarily before realizing that they were on Mete's side of the arena. It would be a challenge to get to them without being hit.

"I see the heir to the KayHan clan crept his way into the final," Mete taunted as the two stood across from one another, awaiting the start of the fight, "It was funny to see a scrawny insect such as yourself emerge victorious from all those fights."

"Funny and ironic that it will happen again in this one." Tu-Kin responded.

Mete laughed.

"I am afraid that is not your decision to make."

After a few more seconds of the finalists staring at one another in disdain, the horn signalling the start of the fight reverberated around the arena. It was time to find out who the true champion of the valley was.

Tu-Kin wasted no time in trying to make his way over to the bow. If he could make his way over to the weapon, the fight would be in his hands. Mete, however, blocked his path. He was far bigger than Tu-Kin, or anyone else in the valley for that matter, and so one could tell that his strength was unparalleled.

Tu-Kin ran toward the bow, fully aware of Mete's presence. As he neared the champion, Tu-Kin could see Mete preparing to strike with his fist. Making full use of his physical training, Tu-Kin rolled under the punch and got back to his feet, preparing to leap away from his opponent. As he took flight, however, he felt a hand wrap around his calf and pull him down. Tu-Kin fell to the ground in a heap, but quickly rolled over, just in time to see Mete's foot crash down beside him. Though the armour he was wearing had slowed Tu-Kin down, he was still quicker than Mete, and he once again rolled out of the way of an attack from the champion, this one a punch that cracked the ground it struck.

Tu-Kin got back to his feet as Mete turned toward him.

"You are quick," He admitted, "But in the arena that means nothing."

"Of course it means nothing to someone as slow and sluggish as you." Tu-Kin teased back.

Having been insulted, Mete charged at Tu-Kin, who slid out of the way at the last possible second. Contrary to his taunt, Mete was much quicker than Tu-Kin had anticipated, though he had an idea in his head. If he could tire Mete out from failing to finish the fight, then he could take advantage of the opportunity. All of Mete's fights had ended in quick to no time, meaning he had yet to experience a long and exhausting fight, something Tu-Kin looked to exploit.

Mete faced Tu-Kin and charged once more. Though Tu-Kin avoided the second charge as well, he was now on the complete opposite side of the arena to the bow. The crowd continued to cheer as Mete punched the stand in frustration.

"Stop running you coward!"

"I am no coward," Tu-Kin replied, "I am fighting with intelligence, something you are unable to do."

Tu-Kin believed that angering the giant would force him to lose his cool, making him vulnerable to someone who was composed. At the moment, Tu-Kin was succeeding in doing so.

"Do not scream for help when I break every bone in your body." Mete warned as he grasped a sword that lay on the ground beside him.

Mete wielding a weapon presented danger. He was not one to hold back in battle, and now that he was angry while in possession of a sword worried Tu-Kin. He needed a shield, and fast.

Tu-Kin turned and ran, feeling the thuds of Mete's own footsteps behind him as he did so. The shield was positioned to the east of the arena, leaning against the stand while reflecting the burning sun in the sky. Tu-Kin changed his direction to the east, making sure to not lose his balance. He eventually made it to the shield and grabbed it, quickly turning and raising it. A clash of metal echoed around the arena as Mete's sword crashed down against the shield. The force of the impact caused Tu-Kin to stumble, but he managed to stay on his feet. He stepped back as he deflected Mete's strikes, each one harder than the last.

"That shield will not save you forever!"

Mete may not have been smart, but he was correct in that regard. If Tu-Kin continued to bear the brunt of his sword, his resistance would falter. Fortunately for him, he had been keeping track of where now was in the arena, and had slowly been making his way over to the bow while blocking Mete's strikes. As he reached his weapon of choice, Mete lifted his sword up and plunged it downward. Tu-Kin leapt backwards and avoided the sword, which dug deep into the ground due to the sheer force of the strike. This was the opportunity that Tu-Kin had been waiting for.

As Mete gripped the sword and pulled it back out of the ground, Tu-Kin wrapped the guige of the shield around his left shoulder and grabbed both the bow and the quiver of arrows, placing the latter around his right shoulder. He quickly took one of the arrows out of the quiver and placed it on the bow. Wasting no time, he pulled the bowstring back and let go. The arrow whistled through the air, but Mete had managed to regain control of the sword, and struck the arrow in the air, splitting it into two.

"You dunce," He yelled, "How do you expect to hurt me with that stick?"

While it was true that Mete was wearing armour, the protection did not shield every part of his body, slim gaps between the sheaving were apparent across the champion's arms and legs. Tu-Kin had found his new targets.

These targets, however, were much smaller and continuously moved as Mete looked to finish the fight. It would be a much harder task to succeed in compared to his training. Tu-Kin let one more arrow fly, this one bouncing off of Mete's chest armour, causing a clear but harmless cut across it. The giant grinned as he walked toward Tu-Kin, confident in his opponent's inability to pierce his armour. Despite the long odds, Tu-Kin continued to fire arrows while avoiding the sword, each one soaring as if to hit one of the gaps before being heartbreakingly swatted away by Mete's weapon or colliding with his impenetrable armour.

Mete laughed again as he stalked his opponent.

"What a waste of arrows they were and what a waste of space you are."

Tu-Kin reached into his quiver one more time and felt nothing but air. His heart sunk temporarily before his finger grazed a piece of pointed metal. It was the final arrow. He had one more opportunity, and he had to make it count.

The two had now set foot in the centre of the arena, the sun and thousands of pairs of eyes beaming down on them. With an evil smile on his face, Mete grabbed his sword handle and repositioned his weapon. In an instant, he pulled his arm back and thrusted it forward, launching the sword directly at Tu-Kin.

The action had taken Tu-Kin, who was in the midst of preparing his final arrow, by surprise. In haste, Tu-Kin leapt to the side, the sword piercing the air beside his now airborne feet. Though he had managed to avoid the attack, he had temporarily forgotten about his possession of the bow while focusing on jumping, resulting in him accidentally letting go of the bowstring.

As he landed on the floor, Tu-Kin shut his eyes. He did not want to catch a glimpse of the shot, embarrassed that he could lose control of the bow so easily. He could not think of any other way to defeat Mete now that his usage of the bow had resulted in failure. Or so it seemed. A large wail of pain rang around the arena, causing Tu-Kin to open his eyes. What he saw amazed him.

Mete was on one knee, grasping at his right knee, which was bleeding. Sticking out of the knee, was the very same arrow that Tu-Kin had inadvertently shot. The arrow had hit its target. Mete had been hurt. Tu-Kin could hear members of the crowd gasp and shout in amazement at the sight.

"I do not believe it, Mete had been wounded, it is a miracle."

Getting back to his feet, multiple thoughts reverberated within Tu-Kin's head. Though Mete was wounded and was unable to move to another position in the arena due to the pain, he had not been defeated, and in order to emerge as victor, Tu-Kin had to get in close to the champion. Having now run out of arrows, he dropped his bow and quiver onto the ground. He had to find a new weapon.

As he looked around the arena, he saw Mete pull the arrow out of his knee and return to his feet.

"You insignificant worm!" He yelled in pure hatred.

Tu-Kin knew he had to be careful. He had learned from his father that a wounded animal was a dangerous animal, and so the success of his shot had caused Mete's anger to reach its boiling point. He swiftly grabbed the sword that Mete had thrown across the arena from the ground beside him and wielded his shield across the other arm. In the centre of the battlefield, Mete stumbled over to a mace and gripped its handle. Though he was drenched in sweat and almost at a loss for breath, Tu-Kin readied himself. It was time for the final clash.

As Tu-Kin approached his opponent, he could feel the weight of his limbs increase with each passing moment. He had used up most, if not all, of his energy during the course of the competition, but he was aware that he could not lose hope at this point in time. He was within touching distance of claiming the crown, and he was not about to give up when so close to his goal.

He finally reached Mete, arousing the crowd to a fever pitch. Tu-Kin made the first move, swinging his sword against Mete's ribcage. The weapon cut through Mete's armour, but was unable to strike his flesh. Pulling his sword out, Tu-Kin raised his shield briskly in order to block a strike with the mace. The two continued to strike at one another, Mete's armour withstanding the sword's strikes while his mace ricocheted off of Tu-Kin's shield. The blows ultimately ended as the two weapons clashed in mid-air, the sword and mace colliding and cannoning off one another, both warriors losing their grips on the weapons and dropping them on the ground. With both of them now disarmed, Mete took Tu-Kin off-guard by grabbing his shield and wrestling it from his grasp. Before Tu-Kin could react, Mete swung the shield and struck the heir of the KayHan clan across the face, sending him sprawling.

Tu-Kin raised his head from the ground as he tasted the blood that had emerged in his mouth. There were now several copies of Mete standing in front of him and the sky had darkened. He had been stunned, and some of his conscious had disappeared, along with his hope.

"You were a fool to believe you had a chance." Mete said with a bloodthirsty glare in his eyes, grabbing the mace from the ground and preparing to finish Tu-Kin off.

Though he hated to admit it, Tu-Kin believed Mete was correct. He had put up an admirable fight, but it was all for nothing. It was time to face the consequences of failing to win.

And that was when a light flashed within Tu-Kin's head. He felt his body strengthen and his heart pump. All of a sudden, he felt as if the fight had only just started. As the mace careened toward him, he rolled out of the way and back to his feet. The weapon buried itself within the ground, a few feet away from a now recovered Tu-Kin.

"What?" Mete asked in shock.

The crowd had become silent. They were once again amazed by the ability of Tu-Kin, who had looked defeated only a few seconds prior. Then the silence was broken.

"Come on my son!" Borge-Han roared from the crowd, "This is your moment!"

The shout caused the rest of the spectators to erupt in noise as Tu-Kin rolled over to the shield and grasped it.

"Have some of your own medicine!" He yelled as he struck the side of it against Mete's wounded knee.

The strike caused Mete to yell in pain once again and brought him down to one knee. With his stance lowered, Tu-Kin closed his fist and blasted it against Mete's chin, sending him stumbling backwards. Tu-Kin repeated the act, causing Mete to turn away from the onslaught. His back now turned, Tu-Kin wrapped his arms around the champion's waist, bent his knees, and, as if he were lifting the tree from the day before, heaved Mete off the floor. With his opponent now in the air, Tu-Kin arched his back and brought Mete down on his head, making sure to avoid hitting his own head as he did so.

The slam took the wind out of Mete's sails and Tu-Kin used the opportunity to clamber onto Mete's back, wrapping his right arm across his opponent's neck and began squeezing it tightly. The champion tried to get back to his feet, but his lack of remaining strength caused him to drop back down to the ground.

"Surrender!" Tu-Kin ordered as he snaked his legs around Mete's own in order to flatten him out and put further pressure on his neck.

The crowd had become unglued at the sight of seeing Mete staring defeat in the face. Their cravings for a new champion were soon satisfied.

"I surrender! I surrender!" Mete yelled, using the rest of his energy to admit defeat and crown a new valley champion for the first time in a long while.

The sound of the horn signalling the end of the fight rung around the arena as the crowd yelled in ecstasy. Tu-Kin let go of the choke and got back to his feet before running around the arena in wild delight. His victory had caused his father to jump down to the arena and join in with the celebrations.

"You did it!" He yelled, trying his best to be heard over the rest of the spectators.

Tu-Kin was speechless at his feat.

"Who is the champion?" His father asked as he smiled lovingly at his son.

The question allowed the moment to finally sink in.

"Who is the champion?" Borge-Han repeated.

"I am!"

"That is my boy!"

The two embraced as the sun shone over the occasion. After a short while the two released their grasp as Borge-Han went over to the crowd.

"My son did it! My son did it! He is the champion!"

It was not a surprise to Tu-Kin to see his father overjoyed at what had transpired. He had claimed the chalice of champions, he had brought honour to his clan, and he had avenged Artuk. What did come as a shock, however, was what happened next.

Tu-Kin felt a hand grasp his shoulder and he turned around to see Mete standing next to him, eye blackened and knee still bleeding. Tu-Kin did not know exactly what to expect from the former champion, but he definitely did not expect what Mete said.

"Congratulations," He said with respect, "You were the better man and you are a true warrior."

As if to add to the surprise, Mete extended his hand, supposedly as a sign of friendship. After a short moment of deliberation, Tu-Kin accepted Mete's offer and shook his hand.

He was soon lifted up from behind, however, and hoisted into the air. Looking down, he could see Teoman was the one bearing his friend's weight on his shoulders.

"How does it feel to be the new champion of the valley?" He asked.

Tu-Kin looked around the arena. The battlefield had now been filled with members of the KayHan clan who had made their descent from the stands to the arena floor. Each one of them were cheering at full volume in admiration of their new hero.

"It feels great." Tu-Kin claimed with a smile.

THE FIRST HUNT

The fallout from the competition had flown by Tu-Kin in a flash. Though he had hoped to get back down to earth following his victory, the rest of his clan prevented him from doing so. No day went by without members of the valley approaching him in admiration, and no day went by without Tu-Kin feeling tired from all the attention. Despite being constantly followed by his fellow clan members, there was only one thing that Tu-Kin could think about as the days went by, and that was fulfilling his wish to lead his own hunting group.

In spite of his success, Tu-Kin had initially felt uneasy about asking for permission from his father, but as the sun continued to rise and fall, he soon became restless and gathered the courage to ask his father. To his surprise, his father had accepted his wish, going so far as to allow Tu-Kin to select the members for his group. The first two choices were simple enough for the valley's champion, and both Teoman and Artuk were happy to tag along with their friend. Tu-Kin, however, was struggling to think of a fourth and final member.

"Are we not enough?" Artuk asked when Tu-Kin brought up the topic to his friends, "You are the leader, I am the smart one and Teoman…"

"I am?" Teoman asked in curiosity.

"Well you are good to be around. You can cheer us on."

"Look," Tu-Kin interrupted, "I still think that we need four people in the group. We would be protected in every direction that way."

"So, who do you have in mind?" Teoman inquired.

"I have an idea of who we should bring," Tu-Kin responded, "But I am going to need your approval."

With that said, Tu-Kin announced who he wanted the fourth member to be.

"Mete???" His friends responded simultaneously, the two of them shocked by the mention of his name.

"Are you crazy?" Artuk replied, "We cannot have him in our group."

"Why not?"

"Are you forgetting what he did to me?"

"I am not forgetting what he did to you," Tu-Kin assured, "I think that you are forgetting what I did to him in the tournament."

A few seconds of silence passed before Teoman spoke.

"If you are fine with him being in the group then I will take your word for it."

With Teoman's approval, Tu-Kin turned to Artuk.

"So, what do you say?"

Artuk waved his hands in frustration.

"Okay, okay, he can be in the group, but do not think for one second that I have forgiven him."

"As long as you can co-exist we should be fine," Tu-Kin stated with a smile, "Now all we need is to get his own permission.

With the decision made, the three of them started their walk toward the centre of the valley, where they were certain they would meet the man in question.

"You want me to join your group?"

The three were now sitting inside a large and warm tent, far bigger than that of Tu-Kin's home. The crescent moon shone through the tent entrance as the fire in the centre burned brightly, generating enough heat to comfort those situated around it.

"I know this is a surprise, but we could use someone who has esteemed battle experience such as yourself."

Mete gazed outside the tent as he thought about the offer, his mother, Aydilge, hastily preparing food beside him.

"Do you think he will say yes?" Artuk whispered over to Teoman who elbowed him as a way of keeping him quiet.

Eventually the former champion stood up and extended his hand.

"You showed me what true strength is in the arena, so it will be an honour to hunt alongside you."

The response was exactly what Tu-Kin had been hoping to hear. He stood up and shook with the newest member of his hunting group.

"Thank you, Mete." He said, grateful.

As the two let go of one another's arm, Mete's mother turned to the group with a smile.

"The food is ready." She announced, holding a large bowl of pilau and boiled meat in one hand and several wooden spoons in the other.

With care, she placed the bowl in the centre of the group and handed everyone one of the spoons.

"Make sure to eat before it gets cold."

The four wasted no time in eating as much as they could. If the smell of the food was great, the taste was even better. Tu-Kin used the opportunity to learn more about Mete, as well as to introduce him to Artuk and Teoman. Though Mete and Artuk greeted one another, Tu-Kin could tell there were still some tensions between the two.

Before too long, the food had been finished, everyone had filled their stomachs to their content. As the four digested their food, Mete broke the silence.

"Where will we go to hunt?" He asked, curiously.

Tu-Kin had thought about several different areas to hunt in since he had first wanted to go hunting. Even though each area had its merits, there was one place that stood out to all the others. A place that Tu-Kin wished to explore, despite its clear danger.

"I wish to hunt beyond the forest, I want to explore the unknown."

The other three looked back in shock.

"But that place is forbidden!" Artuk stated in concern.

"I know, but the only reason it is forbidden is because no one has stepped foot there."

"Why would you even want to hunt there?" Teoman asked, "There are several other places that we are actually allowed to hunt in."

"I know that too, but the thought of hunting there resonates with me. I feel like there is something special beyond those woods."

"The elders of the valley claim dark creatures hide beyond the woods." Mete explained.

"Exactly!" Tu-Kin responded, acting as if the point was a good thing.

"I think you need serious help." Artuk replied.

"And you three will give it to me." Tu-Kin stated.

"That is not what I meant."

"Come on you three, do not you want to find out what is hiding there?"

Nobody responded for a short while, the three considering whether the plan was good or not.

"Are you sure we cannot change your mind?" Teoman asked.

"I am certain in my decision," Tu-Kin affirmed, "If you do not want to join in, then I understand."

The three deliberated for a little while longer before Teoman finally accepted the offer.

"I will tag along with you, two heads are better than one."

"Thank you for going with me."

"Make that three," Mete replied, "The thought of finding out what lies beyond the woods interests me too."

With the offer being accepted by two members of the group, everyone turned to Artuk, who, in turn, looked back before rolling his eyes.

"Fine, I will go too, but only because you will get yourselves killed without me."

"Great," Tu-Kin stated, "We are all set then."

"So is that it?" Teoman asked.

"Before we leave, I need to get something straight."

"What is it?"

"Do not, under any circumstance, tell anybody. Not your father, not your mother, no one."

Artuk put his hand up, as if wanting to speak.

"Yes?"

"Why were you looking at me when you said that?"

"Because if this applies to anyone, it is you."

"What do you mean,? When have I ever told someone a secret?" Artuk responded, completely disregarding his announcement of Tu-Kin's participation in the tournament.

"Just ensure you keep it to yourself." Tu-Kin ordered.

"Okay, I will."

"Good, if everyone is in agreement, then we are all set, make sure to get a good sleep and we will meet at the valley centre early in the morning."

The three guests eventually made their way home after saying their goodbyes, making sure to sleep early in order to wake up in time for the hunt. The wonder of the forest raised many questions within Tu-Kin's head, his excitement at what he could find heightening as he slept.

The sun had only just started emerging when Tu-Kin awoke. He quickly armed himself with his bow, as well as preparing some rope before preparing his horse for the hunt. He rode toward the valley centre and arrived before anyone else had made themselves known. Soon enough, he was joined by the members of his group, each one sat atop their own horse. After the greetings had taken place, the four started their journey toward the forest.

Once they arrived at the forest entrance, Tu-Kin turned to his companions.

"This is the point of no return," He said, "If any of you want to turn back, now is the time."

With everyone certain of their choice to accompany Tu-Kin, the four made their way into the forest. Beams of early sunlight shone through the gaps of the trees that towered over the group as their horses stepped through the bushes that plagued the forest floor. Tu-Kin led the group, eager to find out what was hidden in the unknown.

Though the journey had begun smoothly, the atmosphere soon became tense. Artuk, who was at the back of the pack, had thought meticulously overnight as to how he should get back at Mete for their previous encounter. Though Tu-Kin had forgiven the former champion, he definitely was not ready to do the same. Taking the opportunity that had been presented, Artuk unfolded a bag of small rocks in his hands as his horse continued to clop forward. The rocks were small, and even though they were far from dangerous, they could were certain to cause annoyance, and that is exactly what Artuk was hoping for Mete to feel. Wasting no more time, he flung the first of the rocks toward the back of the giant's head, the stone bouncing off into the nearby bushes. In an instant,

Mete turned around.

"What was that?" He asked.

"What was what?" Artuk replied, acting oblivious.

Mete returned his view to the direction his horse was heading temporarily before he felt another small object hit the back of his head. It was starting to get on his nerves.

"What are you throwing?" He questioned in a raised tone.

Artuk grinned back at him.

"I am not throwing anything."

"Then what is that on your lap?" Mete asked, glancing down at the bag of rocks on Artuk's lap.

The troublemaker lifted the bag and laughed.

"You mean this? This is a bag of rocks."

Mete furrowed his brows before returning his focus to the journey.

"Do not throw anything at me again."

Artuk decided to wait a few minutes before throwing another rock at his companion. He wanted Mete to feel as if he had listened to him before shattering that feeling, hopefully causing him to become outraged. After enough time had passed, Artuk launched another rock at Mete, this one the largest of the bunch, while making sure to gain as much force behind the throw. The stone collided with Mete's cranium with immense force, causing his head to lurch forward as a reaction to the impact. Understandably, Mete turned his horse backward and stared furiously at Artuk.

"What did I just say?!"

"I forgot, sorry, could you repeat it?"

Before tensions could boil over, Teoman turned his horse backward too and situated himself between his two companions.

"Just settle down now," He ordered, "You cannot let past occurrences interfere with this hunt."

"If he does not stop then I will have no choice but to interfere." Mete answered angrily.

"I understand," Teoman affirmed, "But the point still stands, you need to calm down..."

He then turned to Artuk.

"...And you need to stop being a clown."

"Me stop being a clown?" Artuk replied, pointing at Mete, "He is the clown."

"What did you just call me?!"

Teoman sighed in frustration, it would be a challenge to keep those two from angering one another further.

As the ordeal had gone on, Tu-Kin had proceeded further into the woods, not realizing the issue that had been occurring behind him. The area he was now situated in was host to far thicker trees than those near the forest entrance, and the plants seemed to hold more leaves than their thinner counterparts. Despite the limited space, Tu-Kin's horse had no issue navigating the two of them through the vegetation, and the distance between them and the rest of the group steadily increased as time wore on. Suddenly, a distant sound filtered through Tu-Kin's ears and he slowed his horse down in response. The noise continued to sound as Tu-Kin's horse carried him into an open field where the sun was unobstructed. At the opposite side of the field, was a fawn, coloured gold from nose to hoof. Its beauty instantly struck a chord with Tu-Kin, who was captivated by its unique appearance. He had never seen a golden fawn before, and its first impression amazed him. And that was when he remembered.

He recalled Buke handing him the parchment, and how it contained three drawings. The first of them, was that of a golden fawn. Tu-Kin came to the conclusion that the sketch was a depiction of the same creature standing across from him now. The illustration had been labelled as 'sacred' and 'holy', and if the information had come from the elders, than Tu-Kin knew that the details were true. The fawn in front of him was important, but he still wanted to catch it. If the creature was truly sacred, then Tu-Kin had to avoid harming it.

"I might as well tire it while I think of a way to capture it." Tu-Kin said to himself.

His horse strode toward the fawn at his command, chasing it with all its speed. The fawn, as expected, was quick, and managed to avoid being caught up to by Tu-Kin and his steed. As the chase continued, Tu-Kin thought of a way to capture the animal. All he had was his bow, his quiver of arrows, and the long length of rope. Though he had not brought much, the champion eventually came up with an idea that suggested he had brought enough. While his horse continued to run after the fawn, Tu-Kin tightened the end of his rope around the bottom of one of his arrows and placed it on the bow. He quickly pulled the reigns of his horse in order to change the direction of the two, altering their path to cross that of the fawn's. Tu-Kin then aimed his arrow for one of the trees opposite him, gripping his bow tightly in order to gain the perfect shot. The arrow pierced the air before hitting the tree just above its roots. As the rope sailed behind it, Tu-Kin grabbed the other end of the rope just as it flew from his lap and pulled it with all his might, straightening the rope, which now crossed from the tree to Tu-Kin and his horse. The fawn failed to acknowledge the object in time as its front legs struck the side of the rope, sending it hooves overhead and falling in a heap. As it fell, Tu-Kin wasted no time clambering off his horse and sprinting towards the scene. Before the fawn could recover from its trip, Tu-Kin had jumped on top of it. He had caught the golden fawn.

Now that it was caught, the fawn showed little resistance. Tu-Kin leaned over the animal as he pulled the arrow from the tree and untied the knot of the rope, wrapping it around the legs of the fawn in case it decided to try and escape. Caressing it in his arms, Tu-Kin carried the fawn back to his horse, which was receiving a well-earned rest after chasing the baby deer for so long. He was overjoyed at his catch, certain that his father would be proud of his hunt, even if it had taken place in the forbidden part of the valley.

However, as Tu-Kin placed the fawn on the back of the horse, he noticed a strange mist wrapping around his legs. Looking behind him, he could see that the field was clear, yet in front of him, the grass had been covered with an emerald-coloured haze, and it led further into the woods. Ensuring that the rope was tight around the fawn's legs, Tu-Kin made his way over to the other side of the field, where the haze seemed to be coming from. Creeping into the vegetation, Tu-Kin's eyes scanned the area for anything un-natural. A few seconds passed with nothing unordinary occurring before something caught Tu-Kin's eyes. He altered the direction of his view, but there was nothing there. The champion was puzzled, he was certain that he had seen something move. Out of curios-ity, Tu-Kin continued on in the direction he was now focusing on. The mist had started to thicken, and it had begun to cloud his vision. The rustling of leaves was evident from beneath him, his feet making their way through bushes as the haze obscured them from view. Suddenly, a large snap struck the atmosphere, and Tu-Kin turned his head to his right. There was a large opening be-tween the trees, filled with a hue of emerald and purple. Squinting his eyes, Tu-Kin could just about make out a shadowy figure in the near distance. As he made out the figure's four legs, he believed he was looking at the shadow of another deer, maybe even the parent of the fawn he had just caught. But then the top of the fig-ure darkened, and he knew he was wrong. The shadow lacked any sort of antlers, it instead had two large, pointed ears. The outline of the figure was jagged, suggesting it was far hairier than a deer. The thing that had made Tu-Kin's stomach drop, however, was its sheer size. Even though it was a distance away, Tu-Kin still had to bend his head back in order to look at its top. The combination of the large shadow, as well as the wind that had started to blow around him caused his hair to stand on edge. The scene was over-whelming, and though he hated to admit it, it was making Tu-Kin afraid.

Worried that he might be in trouble, Tu-Kin turned on his heels and ran back toward the field, making sure to avoid looking back. Soon enough, he burst out of the woods and returned to the open space, where his horse and the fawn were still waiting. Wasting no time, he clambered onto his steed, placed the fawn around his shoulders, and whipped his horse's reigns, causing the animal to bolt away from the mist. The sight was still clear in Tu-Kin's mind as he exited the field from the other side.

As his horse continued to gallop, Tu-Kin could see the figures of his fellow group members emerge in the distance.

"Oh look, Tu-Kin is here." He could hear Teoman say.

The fear of what could be behind him, however, caused Tu-Kin to continue on his escape, wanting to get out of the woods before coming to a rest. He could hear his friends call out after him as he blew by them, but he avoided stopping. Before long, his horse arrived at the forest entrance, which, thankfully to Tu-Kin, was now the forest exit. He slowly got off his horse and tried to get his breath back, the deer looking at him intently from atop the steed's back.

"Get yourself together, Tu-Kin." He ordered himself as he slapped his cheeks, trying to get the image of the silhouette out of his mind.

He had just managed to divert his thinking back to his success at hunting the fawn when his three group members came into view. They had all made their way after him in a hurry.

Teoman got off his horse and approached his friend with concern.

"Are you okay? You looked pretty scared."

"It was nothing, I was just in a rush." Tu-Kin lied, brushing off his worry.

Artuk soon approached him as well.

"You did hear us call you right?"

"Yes."

"So why did you ignore us?!"

"I told you, I was in a rush."

"A rush? You left us three alone in the woods while you went off on your own little adventure in search of glory. And then when we finally catch up to you, you run off and do not give us a second thought. What if we had died? What if I had died? You probably did not even catch anything worthwhile, this was all a waste of time."

Tu-Kin believed it was only right for him to tell his friends the truth.

"Well, actually..."

"No way!"

Tu-Kin had been interrupted by Mete, who was looking over his shoulder and at the horse.

"You actually caught it."

Tu-Kin could tell that he was talking about the fawn. Both Teoman and Artuk switched their gazes over to the horse, and their eyes widened as they did so.

"You caught..."

"You caught the golden fawn!" Artuk interjected, running over to the animal in excitement, "It is actually golden!"

"How did you do it?" Teoman asked in bewilderment.

"A simple trick with a rope." Tu-Kin claimed.

Artuk had now started holding the fawn in his arms.

"Look at how cute it is," Artuk stated, "I think it likes me."

As he said this, the fawn instantly began growing restless, trying its best to escape Artuk's arms, which it failed to do so due to its tight bounds.

"I do not think it does." Tu-Kin reputed as he regained possession of the fawn, calming the animal as he did so.

"It only tried to escape because it does not know how good my hugs are." Artuk touted.

"Yeah, I doubt that, but anyway, where even were you all? I was not moving that quickly."

"Well, you see…" Teoman started.

"Your friend here started throwing rocks at me," Mete explained, "I got angry and we almost came to blows."

"Good thing too," Artuk stated, "Otherwise I would have knocked you out."

"That is beside the point," Teoman claimed before Mete could get mad at Artuk again, "I had to settle them down, but we should have stayed behind you."

"You two are lucky that we were not in much danger," Tu-Kin explained, "If we were, both of you could have been seriously hurt."

The group took a moment to acknowledge Tu-Kin's words before Artuk spoke.

"So, what are we waiting for? We should bring the fawn to the valley and show everyone," He said with joy, "Tu-Kin, with the help of his most trusted friend, Artuk, captured the sacred golden fawn and made a myth a reality."

"I will do that, but I do not think you deserve more credit than Teoman or Mete."

"Fine," Artuk accepted with a frown, "But we should show everyone anyway."

With the four in agreement, they climbed back on their horses and made their way towards the valley centre.

"Hey Tu-Kin," Teoman asked as the horses clopped on, "What were you going to say before we saw the fawn."

Tu-Kin thought of the silhouette again and changed his mind, deciding that he should keep it to himself.

"Nothing of matter." He replied, as looked on into the distance.

The news of Tu-Kin's catch spread like wildfire. Barely any time had passed when the valley had caught word of the capture of the golden fawn. The occurrence had led to a great celebration throughout Ergene-Kon as everyone gathered in numbers to see the golden fawn in the flesh. The animal had been given a new home in the form of a stable, large enough for the fawn to rest and exercise. Tu-Kin, however, had quickly gotten over his achievement. His mind was solely focused on the misty image that had been forged into his head. He wanted to know more about what he had seen, and he knew exactly who to ask to find out.

"A secret?"

"Yes, I do not want anyone else to know."

Tu-Kin had made his way over to the place where he had uprooted the tree before the tournament. Sitting there when he had arrived, was Buke, the person who he was looking. If anyone was sure about what was behind the mist, it was her. The event had not seemed natural to Tu-Kin, and Buke knew a lot about the supernatural, and so he was eager to tell her what he had seen.

"Okay then, tell me."

Tu-Kin summarized his journey as Buke listened. He could see her interest spike when he got to the part about the haze and the shadow. After taking time to register what Tu-Kin had told her, Buke flicked through her parchments in haste. She quickly scanned one of them and begun asking Tu-Kin some questions.

"What day did you go on the hunt?"

"Two days ago."

"What shape was the shadow?"

"It was really large, I thought it was a deer but it had no antlers and it seemed very hairy."

"And the fog was an emerald colour?"

"Yes, a mix of green and purple."

"And the winds started howling around you."

"Yes."

Having received the answers she was looking for, Buke quickly flicked through her parchments again before pulling out a separate piece. This one had various sketches on it.

"I drew these sketches the night before you went on the hunt," She explained, "I wrote what I could of the elders' teachings, let me just read what I had written."

A few moments passed as Buke did so, Tu-Kin waiting in anticipation for what she was about to tell him. Buke then suddenly let out a gasp.

"What is wrong?" Tu-Kin asked.

"According to what the elders said, the constellations in the night sky warned of an encounter between a hero and a divine creature. They told me that it would happen under the order of Tengri himself. Surely that is what happened when you saw the silhouette?"

"Do you really think so?"

"The stars never lie," Buke affirmed, "Who could the shadow have belonged to?"

As Buke thought, Tu-Kin's mind went back to the parchment he had seen before the competition. He was trying his hardest to remember what the sketch beside that of the golden fawn was. After digging into the deepest parts of his memory, the illustration of a giant wolf appeared in his mind. A wolf. Now that the animal was on his mind, he could see just how well the shadow resembled one. The drawing had been labelled as well, and that was when Tu-Kin realized who he was thinking of, and he could tell that Buke had found out too.

"Asena!" They both shouted in unison.

"Did I really catch a glimpse of Asena?" Tu-Kin questioned.

"We cannot jump to conclusions," Buke claimed, "But almost everything matches up. The constellation, the colour of the mist, the outline and size of the shadow. If what you are saying is true, then I am sure that you saw Asena."

Tu-Kin smiled.

"I have to go there again," He explained, "This time I will make sure to find out exactly what the shadow is."

"You need company, it could be dangerous to go alone. Take Mete with you, I am sure he will help keep you safe."

After considering Buke's offer, Tu-Kin came to a conclusion he saw fit.

"I appreciate your concern, but I have to go by myself. The shadow appeared before me and no one else, yet I decided to run away from it instead of approaching it. Tomorrow, I will go back, and this time, I will face it."

ASENA THE MIGHTY

Tu-Kin made sure to awake before daybreak the next morning. He had not told anyone other than Buke of his plans to venture back into the woods. He armed himself with the same equipment as he did for the hunt and climbed onto the back of his horse once more. Tu-Kin ordered his steed to travel slowly, not wanting to wake anyone nearby this early in the day. Once he reached the forest entrance, however, Tu-Kin whipped his horse's reigns, the steed galloping deep into the woods at its rider's behest. As the two continued deeper into the forest, Tu-Kin thought of his encounter with the shadow. He could not be certain that it belonged to Asena, and he could not be too sure as to how Asena would react to his presence. The questions circled his mind as his horse slowed down to a halt. Looking in front of his horse, Tu-Kin could see that the path had become too narrow for his steed to go through. Acknowledging this, Tu-Kin got off his horse's back, rubbed its neck in appreciation, and resumed his journey on foot.

Now that he was on his own two feet, Tu-Kin had to deal first-hand with the thorns and bushes that obstructed the path. Though he cleared most of them through slashes of his sword, many still scraped against his legs as he walked, tearing through his clothes as they did so. Despite the small pricks, Tu-Kin pressed on. There was no way he was to allow a few thorns to cut his journey short. After a few hundred more steps, Tu-Kin made it to the end of the forest. He had already passed the area where the silhouette had appeared to him, but there had been no sign of it on this trek. His success in getting to the end of the forest, however, allowed Tu-Kin to lay his eyes upon the towering mountains that surrounded the valley.

Situated at the bottom of one of them, Tu-Kin could very clearly see the size of them, and they dwarfed him in comparison. As he looked on, Tu-Kin noticed the winds picking up in speed. Turning around, he could see the very same emerald-coloured mist from his hunt, it had appeared again, and it was just as mesmerizing as it was before. Tu-Kin followed the direction of the haze, this time wanting to ensure that he found out what was causing it. If the fog had appeared, then he believed the shadow was nearby. Believing this, he increased his speed as he followed the mist. It led back into the woods, but no sooner had Tu-Kin re-entered the forest when he found himself exiting it again, this time in a far more open area against the mountains.

In front of him were three giant rocks, and atop the largest one was the figure from before. The sight caused Tu-Kin's heart to skip a beat. It was a wolf, but it was far from an ordinary wolf. It was what his people called a Boz-Kurt, and it had the same size and the same outline as the silhouette, only this time it was in living colour. Snowy-grey fur wrapped around the animal as it stared at Tu-Kin, its blue eyes lay still upon the human that had just appeared. It was clear to Tu-Kin now. It really was Asena. The bright rays of light that were now striking the air reflected off of her moon-like fur as the mist wrapped around her. The winds continued to bellow around them as the two continued staring at each other. It truly was a divine sight, and it had caused Tu-Kin to freeze. He was unsure of what to do. Though he knew a lot of things about Asena, he did not know of how she would react to his presence. There was a very real possibility that she would attack Tu-Kin, and if she did, he knew there would be no escape. He knew of her might, and he was hoping that she would not unleash her power upon him. The feelings within Tu-Kin collided with one another as he stood still, unable to feel anything as he looked at the divine being in front of him.

Then, Asena lifted her head back and let out a howl. The sound shook the mountains behind her as it echoed across the woods, it caused the winds the blow at immeasurable speeds, nearly taking Tu-Kin off of his feet. The howl woke the champion up, he was finally out of the hypnotizing gaze that he had been trapped in, but he was no less afraid. He was certain that he was about to meet his end. He shut his eyes tightly as he thought back to the conversation he had had with Buke. He then recalled the stories that his father had told him when he was a child and the teachings he would hear from the elders from time-to-time.

The awe that struck Tu-Kin when he had learnt about her paled in comparison to the fear that he felt now he was in front of her. Tu-Kin decided to face his fate, and opened his eyes. Asena had turned her attention back to him, but to his surprise, she jumped down and over another, smaller rock beside the two. She looked back, as if signalling for Tu-Kin to follow her, and proceeded down the path. Though he was taken aback by the situation, Tu-Kin quickly scampered after Asena, wanting to know where she was heading. He climbed over the rock to see Asena waiting for him on another rock, this one above ground level. It was clear that she was climbing the side of the mountain. Slowly but surely, Tu-Kin made his way over to the same rock just as Asena leapt upward again. The cycle continued, Asena leading Tu-Kin up the side of the mountain, waiting for him after each jump in order for him to catch up.

The cliff was steep and jagged, causing Tu-Kin to suffer various cuts and bruises along his arms as he climbed after the divine being. His fear had been overcome with curiosity as he climbed. Though he had expected Asena to attack him, she was instead leading him toward an unknown destination. The want to know where they were going made Tu-Kin forget about his bruises and push on through the strong winds.

At various points in the climb, the Boz-Kurt stopped to let out more howls, the wind wrapping around her as she did so. It was clear she was trying to convey a message, but Tu-Kin was oblivious to what exactly she was trying to say. As he continued to ascend, the champion found himself entering the clouds, such was the height of the mountain he was on. Though he found himself going higher and higher, Tu-Kin felt no difficulty in breathing, despite logic suggesting that he would be struggling for air at such a height. Despite the decrease in temperature, Tu-Kin's body remained warm. It was as if Tengri himself had allowed Tu-Kin to reach such a towering height. The cycle was suddenly broken when Asena turned sharply toward the mountain. To Tu-Kin's confusion, she soon disappeared from view. Swiftly following in her footsteps, Tu-Kin found himself looking at a large opening forged into the side of the cliff. It was clearly big enough for Asena to fit through, and so Tu-Kin walked through the gap.

Walking on, he found himself standing atop the mountain, surrounded by the dense clouds that plagued the sky. Though it was foggy, Tu-Kin could just about make out Asena standing a few metres ahead of him. He slowly made his way beside her and marvelled at her size. She turned to face him, her blue eyes shining despite the lack of light, before lifting her head up and howling once more. The winds returned, and they succeeded in clearing the area of the clouds, making the horizon visible in the distance. What was in the distance, amazed Tu-Kin. He could see wide stretches of land, fields and forests not too far off from those within Ergene-Kon.

The sight that shocked him the most, however, was the existence of a village far in front of him. Despite the distance between him and the village, Tu-Kin could tell it was large. There were dark clouds of smoke rising from the tents, suggesting that there were people living in the village. He let out a sigh of happiness. He had found a way out of Ergene-Kon. For centuries, his people had tried to find a way out of the valley, wanting to find a larger place to live their lives.

Despite all of their attempts to find a way out, each search had resulted in failure. And now, right in front of Tu-Kin's eyes, was the world outside of the valley. It was now that he realized what Asena had been trying to show him. She was revealing the passage that the people of Ergene-Kon had sought for so long. Tu-Kin turned towards the divine Boz-Kurt in thanks, but she was now standing back at the gap in the mountain, looking back at him. He understood what he had to do now. It was time to go back to the valley and tell his father of what he had found. It was time for his people to return to their home land.

Wasting no more time, Tu-Kin hurried after Asena, carefully descending back down the mountain once he had ventured back through the opening in the cliffside. As he reached the foot of the mountain, he saw Asena return atop the large rock where he had first witnessed her might. It was clear that she would be waiting here for him again. Taking the bow off his back, Tu-Kin shot his arrows against the trees as he retraced his steps back to his horse.

They would show him the way once he returned. Eventually, Tu-Kin re-emerged in the area he had left his horse, who was laying down on the ground in boredom. As it saw its owner again, however, it sprung to its feet and clopped over to him in happiness. Tu-Kin rubbed its neck and climbed back onto its back. He did not know how his father would react to his story, but he was certain that he could convince him of his encounter with Asena.

As he returned to the forest entrance, Tu-Kin could see his father and several other members of his clan situated outside the camp. Though he was surprised by this, the reason became clear once Borge-Han finally saw him.

"My son, there you are!" He shouted in relief, running over to his son.

Tu-Kin got off his horse and received a tight bear hug from his father.

"The entire valley was searching for you. I wake up to see your bed empty and the horse gone. You should have told me you were going hunting."

"I was not going hunting father, I went for something else."

"Something else? Something that meant you went all alone? Your arms are bleeding and your clothes are torn. You could have been seriously hurt."

"I know father, but I will explain everything to you later. We need to find a place where we can talk by ourselves."

"Why is that?"

"This is really important father."

"Important?"

"It could help the entire valley."

Tu-Kin's words made Borge-Han's eyes widened.

"Do you know of such a place?"

"I know somewhere." Tu-Kin said in certainty

The two made their way over to the large tree that marked the place where Tu-Kin would normally meet with Artuk and Teoman. It was the perfect place for him to recite what he had gone through earlier that day.

"You saw who?"

Certain that he had told his father everything that needed to be said, Tu-Kin was not surprised by Borge-Han's response. He would have reacted the same.

"I know it sounds ridiculous, but I am certain that I encountered

Asena."

Borge-Han stroked his beard as he looked at the sun in the sky, quickly directing his eyes towards the mountains in the distance.

"And you say she showed you the way out of Ergene-Kon?"

"Yes."

Though he wanted to believe his son, Borge-Han was hesitant to do so. His ancestors had failed in trying to find a way out for such a long time that it now seemed impossible to him, even though his son was sure of his words.

"I am not sure," Borge-Han stated, "You may have been suffering from hallucinations. You did venture into forbidden land after all."

"I was not hallucinating father," Tu-Kin replied in defiance, "I saw Asena with my own two eyes, and she showed me how to get out of the valley. If you let me, I can bring you to her. She can show you too."

Borge-Han looked into his son's eyes. Though the story sounded like nothing but a myth to him, he could see the determination in Tu-Kin's pupils. He would have no choice but to let his son take him to the place where he supposedly encountered the divine being.

Before he could react, however, a sharp sneeze sounded beside them. Though it was quiet, in the silence of the moment it was deafening. Turning around, Borge-Han was sure that it had come from behind the tree. Walking around it, he saw three figures crouched behind it, having clearly been eavesdropping on the conversation.

"You three, why are you hiding here?" He asked in a raised voice.

The one in the middle stood up and answered.

"I am sorry but we normally come here every day, we saw you talking with Tu-Kin and decided to approach you without interrupting. We are sorry to have disrupted you."

It was then when Tu-Kin arrived at the scene, emerging from the other side of the tree in a hurry. He was taken aback to see his three friends standing there, sheepishly.

"Teoman? Artuk? Mete? What are you three doing here?"

"It was his fault," Mete stated, pointing at Artuk, "He was the one who suggested hiding instead of just greeting you."

"Hey," Artuk retorted in an attempt to defend himself, "I was just worried about your wellbeing and came to check on you."

"That does not justify hiding behind the tree," Borge-Han explained, "You should have just shown yourself."

"We understand," Teoman replied before Artuk could argue back, "We apologise for not showing ourselves earlier."

After a moment of silence, Borge-Han questioned the group again.

"You were the three that accompanied my son when he captured the golden fawn, were you not?"

"Yes we were." Mete admitted.

"And that is why you should take us along to see Asena," Artuk affirmed, "He is our friend and we can offer him some more protection."

"Your son is telling the truth," Teoman stated, "He is not one to lie."

Borge-Han kept his thoughts to himself for the moment. He could tell that the bond between his son and the three people in front of him was strong, but he was reluctant to bring more numbers than what he thought was necessary. He did not want to risk any of their lives either, and, though he knew the strength Mete possessed, he did not know much about Teoman or Artuk's hunting skills. As he thought, Tu-Kin walked up to him.

"I am sure they will be of great help, father," He claimed, "They will want to see Asena for themselves as well."

With his son's reassurance, Borge-Han finally decided.

"I will accept my son's words, you three can come along if you wish."

Early the next morning, the five set off for the forest on their horses. It was Tu-Kin's third venture into the woods since he had been given permission to hunt, but the hairs on his arms still stood on edge whenever his horse took him into the greenery. Though his steed was now bearing the brunt of both him and his father, who sat behind him, it still darted through the leaves and bushes, with the other three horses all following close behind.

The group eventually came across the space where Tu-Kin had had to continue on foot the previous day. One of his arrows protruded from the bark of one of the trees. He smiled as he noticed it.

"Look over there father," He explained, pointing at the arrow, "That is one of the arrows that I shot to mark the path yesterday."

Borge-Han looked at the arrow and patted his son on the shoulder.

"If that is so, then we must be going the right way."

"We are," Tu-Kin claimed, "But we are going to have to continue on foot, our horses will not be able to go through the forest now."

Looking through the dense vegetation, the group could see that Tu-Kin was right. The bushes were thick, and the same thorns that had made themselves present in Tu-Kin's trek the day before were still snaking across the ground. Dismounting from their horses and stepping into the forest ahead, the group stayed alert.

Though Tu-Kin ensured that he had not been attacked by anything when he went alone, that did not rule out the possibility of a dangerous creature appearing before them during this journey.

The time trickled by as they continued deeper into the woods, the wind increasing in speed as they walked on.

"Are you sure that it is safe to continue?" Borge-Han asked, "This wind feels as if I am being stabbed by thousands of steely knives."

"Do not worry, it means we are close."

Sure enough, the group finally emerged from the forest and stepped out into an open space. The same three giant rocks jutted out of the ground in front of them, and once again, sat atop the largest of the three, was Asena, her fur waving slowly in the breeze. The sight caused Borge-Han to gasp in amazement, while Tu-Kin was sure he saw Artuk's soul temporarily leave his body. Both Mete and Teoman were also taken aback by the presence of the Boz Kurt. Tu-Kin had witnessed the might of Asena before, and now it was time for his father and his friends to experience it too.

Being able to see the divine creature in living colour caused Borge-Han to become rooted to the spot. He remembered the times where he would tell stories to Tu-Kin, each one detailing the extraordinary powers that Asena possessed. Now those stories no longer sounded fictional. What was once a fairy tale had now become reality. His eyes remained attached to the Boz Kurt as it leapt from the top of the rock and landed gracefully on the ground. Out of the corner of his eyes, he could see his son step forward toward the divine creature.

"Be careful son!" He shouted in worry.

Tu-Kin, however, was not worried. He was calm and collected. He had already encountered Asena before, and he knew of her gentle nature toward him. Stepping toward the Boz Kurt, he extended the palm of his hand and pressed it against Asena's head. Though she towered over Tu-Kin, she bent her head in order for the connection to be made, her pupils gazing at the fearless warrior in front of her. Tu-Kin's hand rested against Asena's forehead for a few seconds before he pulled back. The touch now over, Asena leaned her head back and howled in a fashion that Tu-Kin had become accustomed to. In a flash, she turned and jumped over one of the smaller rocks, signalling the same path that she and Tu-Kin had gone on when they first met.

Turning back to his father and his friends, he could see that the expressions on their faces had now loosened. Borge-Han had even started smiling.

"You see, she is showing us the way."

Though the journey up the cliffside had become no easier than it was before, Tu-Kin ascended in excitement. He knew what was waiting for him atop the mountain, and he was certain that it would make his father happy. Fortunately, everyone managed to make their way up the mountain without any serious threat to their health. Eventually the group found themselves in front of a large opening in the cliffside.

"Where did Asena go?" Teoman asked.

"She is through there," Tu-Kin explained, pointing through the gap, "She has a surprise to show all of you."

Tu-Kin allowed his companions to continue before him, wanting them to experience the euphoria of seeing the view atop the mountain before he did. He heard the howl of Asena reverberate around him before long, a sign that the fog atop the mountain had been cleared once again. After waiting for a short while, Tu-Kin made his way through the opening. His father and his three friends were all stood beside Asena, each one laying their eyes upon the land that stretched beyond Ergene-Kon.

They could all see that what Tu-Kin had been detailing was true.

They all had considered finding a way out of the valley a hopeless cause not too long ago. Now, that cause had become possible. The sun continued to smile on them as Tu-Kin took his spot beside his father, who in turn placed his arm around him.

"You really did find it." He said, joyous.

THE FINAL STAND

After taking in the moment and forging the sight into their minds, the group ventured back to the valley. It was clear that a lot rested on Borge-Han's shoulders as they returned home. Tu-Kin knew that his father would need to inform the rest of the valley of the passageway, as well as convincing them that it was real. In addition, the migration of the entire population would definitely prove a challenge, especially when taking all of their livestock. Even if they all managed to leave Ergene-Kon, they would also have to find a place outside the mountain range that had acceptable living conditions. They would also have to beware of their sworn enemies, the Tatars.

"I will host a feast for the valley tomorrow," Borge-Han had told the group, "I will make the announcement then, I forbid any of you to tell anyone of this until then."

Tu-Kin acknowledged his father's order along with his friends. If it was Borge-Han making the orders, no one dared to ignore them. The night flew by in no time, and before long, Tu-Kin found himself seated at one of the many tables scattered around the hall that the banquet was taking place within.

Borge-Han's high status across the valley resulted in a large attendance taking their place in the feast. Each table held several residents of the valley, each one excited for the food and entertainment on offer. The banquet ended up a rousing success, with the food satisfying every mouth that took a bite of it. As the last bits of meat were being swallowed, a group of singers and musicians took centre-stage, entertaining the guests with their impressive talent. Once the rounds of applause at the conclusion of the performances had subsided, Borge-Han stepped to the front of the hall and asked for the crowd's attention in order to make his announcement.

With every pair of eyes and ears directed toward him, Borge-Han then proceeded to describe his journey through the forest in detail, giving specific attention to the might and splendour of Asena. His tale surprised those present to hear them, for they too believed the sight of Asena and the finding of the passageway to be impossible. As a result, most of those inside the hall were reluctant to immediately believe Borge-Han's story, even if he was well-respected among them.

Though the chief of the KayHan clan proceeded to remind the onlookers of their need for a way out, as well as allowing Tu-Kin and his friends to confirm the story, some naysayers remained in the hall.

Sure that this was to happen beforehand, Borge-Han made sure to invite some of the valley elders to the feast, and they were present throughout the entire speech. With his story having been told, Borge-Han asked for the elders to join him at the front of the hall. After they made their way to the chief, they engaged in a conversation with Borge-Han, discussing the legitimacy of the tale, and whether or not it was just a fable. The discourse continued for a short while, the onlookers waiting in anticipation throughout its duration, before the elders turned toward the rest of the hall and declared their support for Borge-Han. As an explanation, they each detailed the prophecies that had been made by their ancestors, as well as the constellations that lined the night skies.

Now that the crowd had been subject to the words of the valley elders, they knew that Borge-Han's tale was true. He had seen Asena with his own two eyes, and there was indeed a way out of Ergene-Kon. Tu-Kin could see the spirits of those within the hall rise. They were now all believers. They believed that there was a way out. They believed that Asena would guide them. They believed that they could reclaim their land.

Though issues of safety concerns and the chances of survival were brought up, the chiefs of the clans soon came up with ways to work around those problems. It was decided that the strongest warriors of the valley would be the first to leave Ergene-Kon. They would be tasked with finding allies across the empire in order to build a strong army, one that was capable of overthrowing the Tatars. This would allow the rest of Ergene-Kon to migrate to their new home.

With everything having been planned meticulously, the preparations began. Tu-Kin led the chiefs of the valley toward the passageway. Once again, Asena waited atop the large rock and, once again, she amazed all who gazed upon her. If there were any lingering doubts in the minds of the chiefs, her presence quickly dispelled them. The Boz Kurt showed the passageway to the chiefs, who were overjoyed at the sight of the pathway. Initially, there were fears that the livestock of the valley would be unable to pass through due to the limited space, but those fears were soon distinguished when Borge-Han realized that the mountain contained an iron core, and a section of it could be melted in order to increase the passage's width. His finding led to him wasting no time in ordering the blacksmiths of Ergene-Kon to melt the side of the iron mountain.

Now that every chief in the valley had set their eyes on both Asena and the pathway, their plan was set in motion. The trees that obstructed their path were cut down. Though the task would have normally taken a while to be completed, the participation of the entire valley meant that all of the obstructions had been cleared before too long. Once the way through the forest had been cleared, the clan were left with enough wood to reach the sky.

The pieces of wood were then positioned around the iron mountains alongside seventy layers of coal. The blacksmiths used all of their expertise to locate exactly where the materials had to be placed, and, with their approval, the wood and coal were set ablaze. The process of melting the iron core took a while, but, after maintaining the intense temperature of the fire for several days, the mountain was finally melted and the path had now become large enough for any creature within the valley to go through. Asena watched over the residents of Ergene-Kon for the entire duration of the process, her divine presence making sure that they were safe during their mission. She was a sign that the valley had been blessed, not only by the Boz Kurt, but by the great Tengri as well.

With the pathway now cleared, it was time for the strongest warriors to go out and implement the plan. Tu-Kin's prowess in the tournament, as well as his finding of the golden fawn and Asena, led him to be declared the leader of the army. He was pleased to see Artuk, Teoman and Mete join him in the mission, and he also recognized a lot of others from the tournament. The night before he was due to set out on his mission, Borge-Han had given Tu-Kin İl-Han's heirloom.

It had been kept safe throughout the generations, and now Borge-Han was entrusting it to his son. As well as the heirloom, Borge-Han handed Tu-Kin the sword of KayHan, said to be the mightiest blade in the entire valley. It had been crafted elegantly, and its size dwarfed any sword Tu-Kin had wielded before. He was honoured to have been given the two most important possessions his father owned, and he made a promise to keep them safe and to use them wisely.

"My son, within you I see a great warrior. There is no question that you are the true heir to the İl-Han empire. It is your destiny to bring our people back to their rightful home. I know that you may feel nervous about bearing the hopes of the entire valley on your shoulders, but we all have complete faith in you, and I am certain that you will restore the pride of our ancestors. May Lord Tengri forever be with you, and I await your success while I tend to those who remain here. You are already a hero, now it is time for you to become a leader."

The day of reckoning having arrived, Tu-Kin waved his goodbyes to his family, sheathed his new sword, climbed onto his horse, and rode off toward the pathway. Though he was ready for the task at hand, there was one more person he came across before he could start the mission. It was Buke, who had been waiting for him a short distance away from the forest. As Tu-Kin rode toward her, he could see she was holding something in her hands. It was a greatbow, with silver inscriptions and much bigger than the one Tu-Kin had used in his practice for the tournament. She handed it over to him

"Take this, may it protect you in all the battles you will fight." She said.

She wished him the best of luck for the task he was about to undertake. As a token of gratitude, Tu-Kin gave her his own bow before once again setting off for the passage. The squad of soldiers left Ergene-Kon with the hopes and prayers of the valley leading them on. They knew of the blessing that had been placed upon them by Tengri, and with the protection of Asena, they knew they could not fail.

Not long after they entered the empire, the army were aware of the lack of integrity surrounding the Tatars' rule. They had apparently failed to keep a lot of their promises to the other clans within the empire, and this had caused their so-called 'allies' to become infuriated at their lack of honour.

This was exactly what Tu-Kin and his army had hoped for, and, using İl-Han's heirloom and KayHan's sword to prove his right to the throne, he successfully convinced the disheartened clans to join his cause. As a result of the change in allegiances, conflicts arose across the empire, causing the rule of the Tatars to weaken with each passing defeat. As well as weakening the Tatars' rule, Tu-Kin and his army were able to aid other smaller tribes in thriving after the dictatorship of their rulers had caused great harm to them.

After several months of conflicts, the army had managed to push the Tatars' rule to the verge of extinction. They were vulnerable, and Tu-Kin could tell that it was time to notify his father of his army's success. He sent the message back to the valley, and those who had stayed in Ergene-Kon were more than ready to move out. During the conflicts within the empire, Borge-Han had set about preparing the valley for war, training them physically alongside Bayhan to ensure that they had unparalleled strength by the time the invasion was to take place.

Now that the go-ahead had been given, it was time for them to invade. Rushing down from the mountains, they looked to be descending from the skies to onlookers within the empire. The sight led to the new army naming themselves the Gok Turks, the sky people. Though they had been divided into different troops, the army were strong physically, and even stronger mentally, knowing that Tengri would be smiling down upon them whenever they rode into battle. They held flags, the sky blue-coloured cloths waving elegantly in the wind, each one embroidered with the silhouette of Asena, striking fear into anyone who clashed with them in battle.

The army invaded the empire with a ferocity that had never been seen before. The forces overpowered the weakened Tatars and their allies, whose rule came to an end in spectacular fashion. The success resulted in major celebrations across the empire, not only from those who had resided in Ergene-Kon, but also from the people that had been subject to the Tatars' cruel treatment for several eons. It had taken the valley a long time, and many failures beforehand, but they had at last reclaimed their homeland. They had overthrown the rule of the Tatars and freed those who had been forced to deal with their harsh treatments. They had realized KayHan's dream.

With the war a success, Tu-Kin was crowned the true heir to the empire. A grand coronation was held for the boy who had defied all expectations to achieve what was thought to be impossible. The elders held special ceremonies for the people of the empire to give their thanks to both Tengri and Asena for giving them the strength and determination that they had needed to succeed.

The empire was now named the Turkic Khaganate, and, although the residents of the valley had left, they had not forgotten about the importance that Ergene-Kon held in their survival. It had been their temporary home for the time they had spent away from the empire, and it was not about to be lost in the memories. It was labelled the holy land of the Turkic Khaganate. Special prayers would take place within the valley, and it was now considered a sacred place. The first Turkic Khaganate had been formed. After millennia of separation from their true home, the Gok Turks had regained their homeland, and at the centre of the accomplishment, was Tu-Kin the brave. A boy that had become a hero, and was now to be regarded as a warrior for generations to come.

AFTERWORD

Ergene-Kon means so much to the Turkic people that walk the earth today. It is a place that saved a handful of humans from the brink of destruction, and gave them a chance to continue their lives and lineage in peace. The valley holds a special place in the hearts of so many Turkics, who would not be here today if it were not for the history changers that found Ergene-Kon all those milennia ago.

The tales of Ergene-Kon have been told for nearly two-thousand years within the Turkic region, but I believed it was time for the rest of the world to know about them as well. I always felt that the one thing missing from the fables was a hero, one to truly lead the Turkic people of the time. This is what led me to create Tu-Kin. I believe that his addition completes the story, and allows for a greater bond between story and reader.

I thank all who aided in the creation of this book, and I know Tengri himself will be watching over all of you, ensuring that you are safe with his blessing.

Printed in Great Britain
by Amazon